"What I'm going to show you is knuckles and blood—
your blood . . ."

Clint stared at the gun in his hand. He had a sinking feeling that about the only way he had a chance of stopping this fellow was to shoot him in the knee. That seemed pretty drastic and yet . . .

The man charged again. Only this time, he was expecting something tricky and when the Gunsmith tried to trip him, he jumped the outstretched leg, threw his big arms around Clint, and drove him into the ground. He was fifty pounds heavier and a damn sight stronger. He got both knees on Clint's chest and then he reared back to punch his head off. Clint palmed his gun and drove it into the man's face— the blacksmith's nose broke with a popping sound.

**Don't miss any of the lusty, hard-riding action
in the Charter Western series, THE GUNSMITH**

And coming next month:
THE GUNSMITH #50: WHEN LEGENDS MEET

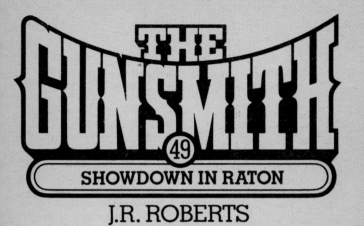

THE GUNSMITH

49

SHOWDOWN IN RATON

J.R. ROBERTS

CHARTER BOOKS, NEW YORK

THE GUNSMITH #49: SHOWDOWN IN RATON

A Charter Book/published by arrangement with
the author

PRINTING HISTORY
Charter edition/January 1986

ISBN: 0-441-30953-4

Charter Books are published by The Berkley Publishing Group,
200 Madison Avenue, New York, New York 10016.
PRINTED IN THE UNITED STATES OF AMERICA

ONE

The Gunsmith was sitting in the White Elk Saloon the day he received the urgent message from old Pete Haywood. It was a cold winter day in the Wasatch Mountains of Utah and Clint Adams was warming his feet beside a potbellied stove that was so hot it glowed cherry red. There was a pretty young woman named Bella upstairs hoping he'd come up to visit but Clint was content to remain where he was for the moment. Right down here he had the best seat in the house and if he left it, there'd be someone else eager to take his place so near the stove. There was not a warmer or more congenial place to be anywhere in American Flat.

The unwritten rule was that it was all right to get up and take a leak or get a drink and still keep your place in the circle, but if you got restless and just wanted to stretch your legs, go scratch your dog or horse, or love a woman, then you forfeited your chair and had to hang around and wait for another turn, which might not come until early the next morning.

It was a fair enough arrangement and one that avoided a whole lot of trouble. Clint had gotten downstairs early that morning and here it was ten o'clock. The wind was whistling outside and it looked like it might even snow for the first time this season.

When old Orly Walker straggled in, he was smart. He said, "Clint, there's an urgent letter for you down at the postmaster's. Better go get it right now."

Clint frowned. If he did, he might never get his chair back. "How do you know it's urgent, Orly?"

" 'Cause it says so on the envelope."

Clint scowled. "There's not a whole lot of folks even know that I'm here in American Flat. Maybe it's not even for me."

"Got your name on it. Right under the word *urgent*. Postmaster says it's yours all right. Aren't you going to go get it?"

All the other men around the potbellied stove were watching him with a great deal of curiosity. They could read his mind, understand how reluctant he was to give up his place in the warm circle.

"Well," Orly said, growing impatient, "aren't you going to get it?"

Clint pulled his Stetson down low over his eyes. "Maybe just a little later. Did you happen to read on the return who sent it?"

"Yep."

Clint waited. Orly was being his usual obstinate self and he was irked because Clint hadn't jumped up and lost his chair. "Well, are you going to tell me or do I have to get up and stick your head in the damned stove and burn off what little hair you still have left?"

The threat brought some guffaws from those around the stove but there was enough of a threat in the Gunsmith's voice to warn Orly that he was getting himself out on thin ice.

"It's from a man named Pete Haywood down in Raton, New Mexico. That's all I know, damn it. That and that the letter is marked . . ."

"I know—*urgent*."

"Yeah, but you sure don't seem to care that your friend is in trouble."

"Thanks, Orly. I'll send a boy for the letter soon as one moseys in here."

"They're all in Miss Potter's school. Won't be none here until this afternoon. Some urgent!"

Clint managed to hide his smile. Orly had figured he had the best seat in the saloon and now he was still out in the cold.

"Sorry," Clint said wryly.

Orly shuffled off. He was a grumpy, old, former drunkard who'd dried out a few years ago and now did odd jobs around the town in good weather. Clint liked the crusty son of a bitch but he could get a little pushy at times and seemed particularly irritable when the weather got real cold as it was today.

"You were a little tough on Orly, Clint."

He glanced sideways at Pat Sinclair, a local rancher who enjoyed spending his time in town a whole lot more than out at his ranch. Clint had seen Mrs. Sinclair once or twice so he could understand why Pat was around here so often.

"Orly can wait a few more hours before he takes my chair," Clint said, wiggling his toes in his warm boots, and yawning. "I'm too comfortable to get up right now."

He closed his eyes and thought back to the day when Pete Haywood had saved his life down in New Mexico. It had been a day much like this one. He'd just cleaned up a nasty bunch who'd beaten up drunks late at night and rolled them for their money. Then they had moved on to extorting so-called protection money from local storeowners.

Pete owned a saloon. When the gang had tried to force Pete into paying them for protection, he'd beaten hell out of their ringleaders, and from that moment on his life had been in grave danger. Someone had finally winged Pete and with his gunarm in a sling, he was in bad trouble. Since he had been friends with Clint for many years, he wrote to him.

Clint smiled. Come to think of it, Clint mused, he'd

scrawled the word *urgent* then, the same as he had done now. And it had been urgent. One of the gang would have soon killed him if Clint hadn't arrived. He'd wasted no time in seeking them out and gunning down the worst three. The other two, a pair called the Tater brothers, had fled into the New Mexico hills.

Clint had ridden out of Raton a few days later heading down toward Laredo, Texas, where he figured he might just winter. It would be warm there, and he knew a couple of real pretty ladies who'd be happy to extend him some of that city's best hospitality.

Eight miles south, however, the Tater brothers had set up an ambush. They couldn't have missed either, for Clint had been forced to ride his big black gelding, Duke, through a narrow pass in the mountains.

He would never forget how uneasy he'd felt down in that pass—how the high rock walls had seemed to lean in on him and how he figured it would be a perfect place for ambush.

Pete Haywood had felt the same way. Not having had a chance to warn Clint before he left town, he and his little boy Zeb had ridden out after him and rode hard to beat him to the pass. They'd anticipated an ambush, and when the brothers poked their rifles out from the rocks and started to sight in on Clint, old Pete and his boy Zeb opened fire. They riddled those two ambushers before they could get off a single shot.

Then, Pete and Zeb rode down into the pass and said good-bye. It had been a cold, blustery afternoon and they'd shared a full bottle of whiskey and Pete had even let his son have a swallow or two. It had been one of the best farewells in Clint's memory and one he'd always treasure. He'd saved Pete; then Pete and his young boy had returned the favor. Friends couldn't do much more than that for each other. Friends like that were never forgotten.

Clint fidgeted in his chair. I wonder what Pete is in trouble over this time? Wonder if he still owns that Hot Lizard Saloon. Hell of a name but that's about what his whiskey tasted like going down, ground up lizards mixed in with hot red peppers. He still shuddered to think about it even though it sure could warm a man on a cold day like this.

Pete had been a pretty fair hand with a gun. And a hell of a fistfighter. He'd lower his scarred old head and come wading into a crowd just swinging from the rafters to the floor and clearing out anything or anyone who stood in his way.

Clint frowned. Sure hope Pete is all right. Must be at least sixty or sixty-five by now. He'd lived a hard life. Clint sat up straighter and he had an awful thought—what if old Pete had died and was fixing to get buried? He'd have wanted Clint to be there as his best friend, but . . . well, they'd have had to buried him by now. Even in this cold weather, he wouldn't have kept very well above ground. No, Clint decided, it wasn't a funeral invitation. Had to be something else.

But what? And how did Pete find out that he was here in American Flat, Utah? Must have gone to a lot of trouble to track him down. Pete wasn't one to go to much trouble unless there was really something serious the matter.

The Gunsmith couldn't sit still in his chair. Curiosity was like an itch that needed—demanded—to be scratched right now. He gripped the arms of his chair, eased his feet back from the stove, and climbed to his feet.

A number of the gents around the fire were having trouble keeping from smiling. It was as if they'd known all along that he couldn't bear the suspense of a letter that was marked *urgent*. But the worst part, the most humiliating part was turning around to stand face to face with toothless, practically hairless old Orly. The man was grinning from ear to ear and his rheumy blue eyes were now glistening with what could only be described as triumph.

It was all Clint could do to keep from laying hands on the

old fool. ''There better be a letter there,'' he warned. ''If this is one of your tricks, I'll . . .''

Orly eased by him and sat down in Clint's chair like a hen easing down on a nest of eggs—and he looked about as satisfied, too. ''It's there all right,'' he said. ''And it's marked *urgent* just like I said. I'm not stupid enough to dream up something that clever, Gunsmith.''

''Huh?'' Clint frowned. ''Never mind. It just better be important is all,'' he groused as he headed to the door.

Back around the fire, the ring of toe-toasters did not even wait until he stepped out into the icy morning air before they began to start laughing. Sometimes, Clint thought, a man got no respect at all.

TWO

Outside, the wind was moaning through the trees, and the horses tied to the hitching rail were all bunched up as close as they could get to each other for warmth. Clint wasn't sure, but he guessed the temperature was still well below freezing, and when he passed a frozen water trough, he was sure of it.

American Flat was a town of about four thousand and was mostly dependent upon ranching and logging, in that order. The logs were cut and freighted down to Salt Lake City or Ogden and the mountain roads bred the best and the bravest freighters in the country. There had been a few local gold strikes hereabouts, but they'd not lasted. In a way, that was fine because boom towns dependent upon mining came and went almost as frequently as the seasons.

But a town like this that didn't grow too fast and relied upon beef and lumber for its existence could count on being around for quite a while. It was a real pretty setting too, lots of green forests to walk and mountain streams to fish in good weather, even a couple of lakes to swim in if a man liked that sort of thing. But the winters were rough at almost seven thousand feet and Clint had been thinking about hightailing it on down south, perhaps to Tucson or Phoenix where the sun shone warm even in January.

Maybe, he thought, I'll be going to Raton, New Mexico, instead. Not as warm as I might have wanted, but warmer by far than eastern Utah. Trouble was, Bella was going to take

7

his leaving hard. But on the other side of the coin, there would be no less than a half dozen of Bella's old boyfriends that would be mighty glad to see the Gunsmith hit the trail south. They'd probably all get together and console poor Bella, and then they'd have a hell of a good time.

The letter was waiting just as Orly said it would be and the postmaster was as nosy as Clint had remembered him to be from the last time he'd received a letter.

"Trouble, Mr. Adams?" he asked almost hopefully. "It's marked *urgent* all across the front. I told old Orly he better scoot across the street and hunt you up. Said it must be pretty important to be marked up that way."

Clint took the letter. "Must be," he said, studying it.

"Orly said it was a woman wrote it and that Bella was going to be mad as hell when she heard about this woman. Is she really in bad trouble?"

Clint scowled. "It's a him. Just like it says on the return. You must have read that."

"Yeah, I did, but sometimes a pretty woman might put that on a letter to fool another woman. Been done a hundred times before."

"Well, not this time. Pete is an old friend."

"What does he want?" the postmaster asked bluntly.

Clint shoved the letter into his coat pocket and grinned with malicious delight. "Kind of makes a fella wonder, doesn't it?" Then, before the postmaster could voice his displeasure, Clint walked out the door.

He started back toward the saloon but saw two or three of the locals gawking at him, probably waiting to see what the urgent letter was all about. Clint angled off toward the stable. He could read the letter to Duke, who wasn't so damned nosy and would have more of a personal stake in it than anyone else in this town.

He bulled through the wind and then had to shoulder the

barn door open to get inside. It was really blowing hard and it felt as if it were right off the North Pole. Inside, he stomped his feet to get them warm and rubbed his hands together. Little Shorty Grubb, the stablemaster, was pitching hay to the horses. He sat his pitchfork down and waved. ''Howdy, Mr. Adams. Real pisser of a day, ain't it!''

''Sure is.'' He headed toward Duke's stall but Shorty stood in his way.

''You open that urgent letter yet, Mr. Adams?''

Clint could not believe this town! Was he the only man who ever got an urgent letter? The only one who held to the apparently outdated notion that a man's mail was his own business and not everyone else's?

He yanked the crumpled letter out of his pocket and skirted Shorty to enter the stall and pat his horse affectionately. ''Duke is looking good, Shorty. You've been taking fine care of his coat.''

''Well, thank you! What's the woman from Raton who has trouble expect you to do about it? Hell, you haven't seen her in a couple of years! I can't see how her baby could be yours in the first damn place. Don't let her rope you into marriage like this. She ain't worth riding clear down to Raton in this weather!''

Clint stared at the stableman with a mixture of astonishment and disbelief. He guessed you never could tell what kind of an imagination a man possessed inside his head. Shorty, for example, was a little gimpy fella who'd probably never left his part of the country and had curried about a million horses in his life and hadn't done a whole hell of a lot else. But it was obvious that he journeyed fast and far in his mind. Probably took a look at every man who left his horse in his care, judged the man and his outfit, and then let his imagination take wing. In a way, it was kind of remarkable. The little fella's rich imagination gave him all the pleasures and none of the hardships, dangers, and disappointments. But imaginations, just like men and horses, needed to be fed or they'd starve.

"Shorty, I tell you," he said, making a quick and probably rash decision that would come back to haunt him later, "if she swears it's my kid, I'll just have to take a look at the little jasper and then decide."

"Hard to tell if it's yours at that age. Don't see how you could at all," came the dubious reply.

"Well," Clint drawled, "if it's red or yellow, brown or black, that'd be a dead giveaway, wouldn't it?"

"She'd . . ." He blushed. "She'd do that to you!"

"She might," he said, pulling out the letter and tearing it open. "She's a mighty wild, wild woman."

"Wow!" Shorty looked away and when his eyes got that faraway look, Clint reckoned his imagination was working overtime and he was down in Raton himself.

Clint smiled, and then he opened the letter and read it.

Dear Gunsmith,
  I know the letter says urgent *and maybe it is and maybe it isn't but I need you down here right away. Don't run the shoes and fat off Duke, but get here before Christmas if you can, and watch out for trouble on the way down. Looking forward to seeing you again.*
                                        Your old pardner,
                                        Pete Haywood.

"Grain Duke extra heavy this morning, then saddle him, and pack food and grain for us both to take along on the trail to New Mexico. I'll be leaving before noon."

Shorty snapped out of his daydream though it was easy to see he didn't want to. "Sure thing, Mr. Adams! Is it . . . a boy or a girl?"

What the hell, Clint thought, why not give the man some-thing juicy to really have fun with this winter? "We don't know yet. You see, it hasn't been born. The Contessa isn't expecting the baby until Christmas. She's calling all of us in to have a lottery and the winner gets to marry her and keep the kid."

"Wow!" Shorty swallowed hard. "She must be even prettier than I imagined. And a real pistol, too," he giggled with a sly wink.

Clint winked back at him. "Any time, place, number, color, shape, or size."

Shorty mopped his brow though the air was freezing. "How many this time? For the lottery, I mean?"

Clint pulled out his letter and peeked inside. He felt like a real sidewinder for doing this, but he'd gone too far to back out now. The whole town was going to go crazy when Shorty spread the word.

"I don't exactly know how many of us there is. But written in big letters right beside my name there's number seventy-four. You think that means . . ."

"Oh, wow!" Shorty gasped. "She is amazin'!"

Clint headed for the door. When he bulled back outside, Shorty was already far, far away.

But Bella wasn't and Clint owed her the honest truth and a fond farewell. And if he didn't get up to her room before Shorty returned to reality and hit the door of the White Elk Saloon with his mouth running faster than his legs, Bella wouldn't listen to Clint at all—she might even kill him.

THREE

Bella Johnson was a good woman gone a little bit bad. She had been raised by a strict, Quaker family in Pennsylvania, but when she'd been caught holding hands with a boy her own age, her father had called her a whore and beaten her with a whip. A year later, she'd been caught by a neighbor kissing that same boy on the lips and rather than face an even worse punishment, she'd run away from home. She'd walked all the way to McKeesport and then met a sweet-talking young horsetrader who convinced the still virgin Bella to give him more than kisses for a ride west clear to St. Louis, Missouri. By the time she'd reached that Mississippi River town, she guessed she was a whore just as her father had said because the man never once asked her to marry him and she'd done things to his body she never dreamed were possible. Even more sinful, she'd liked doing all of them. She had loved him, so that had made some difference, didn't it?

Bella was long on pride—maybe too long on it for she refused to beg for respectability, even though she thought she would die of shame and a broken heart. Her first man had taught her many things, however, and besides the ones about how to pleasure a man in the night, he taught her that she must never give her heart away again.

But she had with the Gunsmith.

Now, as she sat on the bed and stared at Clint, she felt a deep disappointment that he was going to leave her. And yet she also sensed relief because the longer he stayed the harder it would be when the day finally came and he said good-bye. And he would say good-bye—Clint had made that very clear right from the beginning and she respected him for it. He was a giver as well as a taker, a man who thought about how to please a woman as well as how to be pleased. He never got drunk or mean as men often did; he was a gentleman. Yes, that description best suited the Gunsmith. A gentleman.

He showed her the letter because he wanted no doubts in her mind about why he was leaving so suddenly for Raton. Then, he told her the story he gave to Shorty Grubb and they laughed hard together.

Bella sighed. "Well, damn it, I always knew this day would come, but I thought I'd maybe get to keep you for the winter."

"Think of it this way," Clint said, looking at her long black hair and admiring the way it shone in the morning sunlight filtering through the curtains, "There are damn few good women here and a lot of lonely men that need some honest loving. Besides, you need to earn some money, Bella."

"I never thought about it with you," she said.

Bella was dressed in a man's red flannel longjohns. They were too big and not especially becoming, yet they could not hide the rich roundness of her ample figure. Her breasts were big and luscious, about the size of cantalopes and much sweeter. Clint loved those breasts and sometimes when Bella had a little champagne in her, she liked to do a strip dance to the sound of the honky-tonk piano music that would filter up to her room. She could wiggle and shake so that those breasts of hers would go every which way and then she'd make them rotate in opposite circles and he'd just go hard with desire. He'd always end up jumping her before the dance was over and she really got into the bumping and grinding.

And after you jumped Bella, well, that was the best part of all. She liked to wrestle around a little. Bella was strong; she'd worked hard all during her childhood on that Quaker farm, milking cows and hauling wood and water. She had muscles under that smooth white skin of hers and she could fight like a wildcat or buck you off like a horse when she wanted.

"It says"—Bella had reached over and pulled the letter out of his pocket—"it may or may not be urgent, Clint. Couldn't you . . . no. I guess you couldn't stay a few more days. Besides, Christmas isn't that far off."

"No, it isn't." Clint dug into his pocket. "I've got a Christmas present for you already, Bella."

He made her close her eyes and then he took out the gold necklace with the big nugget and fastened it around her neck. The nugget was tear-shaped and tears shone in her eyes when she opened them and saw the present.

Bella was a strong woman, one who never lost control of her emotions because she'd been taught not to all the years of her Quaker upbringing. But inside, she was just as soft as could be, and it was all she could do to say, "I haven't gotten you anything yet, Clint."

"Yes, you have," he said, unbuttoning the top of her flannel pajamas.

She swallowed noisily, raised her chin, and said, "That's right, Clint. I can at least give you this for a going away present. Give it to you so good that maybe someday you'll come back for a visit."

Bella let him unbutton her all the way. Then, she slipped out of her pajamas and slowly unbuttoned his shirt. She kissed his chest and ran her tongue over his nipples and then unbuckled his gun and tossed it on the bed. She knew exactly what he liked and this time she was going to make it better than ever, give him all he could stand until he was moaning with pleasure and aching to unleash his seed deep into her body. Then, she'd make him wait just a few excruciating minutes longer.

She liked the way he was built—he was not stocky and with big bulky slabs of muscle. Rather, he was hard, long-muscled and graceful. He was built, she thought, the way a man ought to be built and the way the hard-struggling Quaker men were not.

Bella unbuttoned his pants and, staring straight into his eyes, slipped her hand down into his crotch and cupped him. "You are mine for the next few hours. And I'm not letting you leave American Flat until I've given you something to remember. Do you understand?"

He grinned and nodded.

She reached up a little and took his already hard cock in her hand and kneaded it gently with her fingers. She could see his eyes go a little glassy with the anticipation of even greater pleasure. If he could only stay, only love her, she . . . Bella pushed the thought away and roughly pulled down his pants. He sat down on the edge of the bed and she knelt before him.

She bent over and took him in her mouth quickly and almost fiercely and sucked him hard for a few moments before rearing her head back and tossing her long black hair. She smiled at the look on his face and pulled his boots and then his pants off and began to rub a forefinger around the inside of his thighs.

He groaned. "Oh, Bella, you are really going to make me work for this last one, aren't you?"

"You are a beautiful, beautiful man, Clint Adams. And I'm going to miss you at night."

Before he could answer, she took his cock in her mouth and then lowered her head so that her long dark hair cascaded down to cover him and then she began to eat him like a piece of licorice candy. She loved doing this to the Gunsmith, loved feeling the way his body responded and knowing how much he enjoyed it. Bella always thought that if she had any shortcoming with this man in bed it was that she got too frenzied herself.

When he was getting close to a climax, Bella stopped long enough to climb up and straddle him. Slowly, with her torso erect, her long hair cascading down from her shoulders, breasts and belly gleaming with the mist of perspiration from her passionate efforts, she moved her pelvis around and around in a slow ellipse. After five minutes, she began to move with greater force and speed.

The Gunsmith intertwined his fingers behind his head and watched her intently. "I can't ever have imagined you the wife of some staid Quaker, Bella. You'd never have lasted. There's too much woman inside of you that needs to be appreciated. Way too much! Any man would be lucky to have you."

Her eyes were closed and she was rocking faster and faster. Her shapely hips were going around and around in circles and now she let go of him and sat down hard. "Ooohhhh!" she moaned as her body begin to piston up and down on him faster and faster.

Suddenly, she was hunched and bucking wildly. Clint almost lost control himself. He grabbed her and pulled her down, feeling her stomach trembling and her hands digging into his buttocks as if she could pull him almost through her.

He waited until she was breathing more slowly and then he said, "Now, it's my turn."

She giggled. "You're ready to go right now, Clint. You're so big and hard you must be aching to keep from letting it go inside me."

He tried to tell her that he was not, that he would decide, not her. He started to pull back but her legs locked themselves around his lean hips and Clint knew that he was finished.

There was nothing to do but go with the mounting fever that was driving his loins like pistons.

"All right," he breathed hoarsely as he exploded inside of her, "take it, Bella. Take it all!"

It was hard to leave such a woman, harder than he'd thought, and the cold wind he and Duke faced made the parting no easier. All the boys gave up their seats around the potbellied stove to come outside to shake his hand. Even old Ormly.

Shorty Grubb cried, "You sure don't have to marry her, even if she does pick number 74! You don't have to, Mr. Adams!"

"I'll remember that," Clint shouted over the wind.

He looked at the men he'd been swapping chairs and lies with for the past month or so. "You boys take care of Miss Bella. Anybody tries to hurt her, or rob her, you know what to do. And if you can't do it, then you find a way of letting me know and I'll come back and kill the man who mistreats her. Understand?"

They all nodded. The Gunsmith was not a man to make idle threats. The word would get around, but most everyone knew that Bella could handle herself pretty well.

Clint leaned down and kissed Bella. "You take care of yourself. I'll be back again some day. But in the meantime, if you find some handsome young buck who falls in love with you, give him a chance. You might even fall in love right back. Get married. Have some strong, beautiful kids. Wouldn't be all bad, you know."

She nodded. "I'll think it over, Clint."

Something in the way she said it made Clint feel good. Made him feel that maybe he'd opened her up inside the heart and that she might dare to love again, to try again with someone new. That horsetrader who'd not wanted to marry her in St. Louis was a damn fool. He'd lost the best woman he'd ever have a chance for. Now, Clint was leaving her, but the hurt that had once been in her eyes was gone. Clint had a hunch that he'd find Bella someone's faithful wife next time he passed through.

So he reined Duke east toward the higher mountains and waved good-bye. And when he got to the end of the wind-blasted street, they were still standing out in the cold waving at him and that made him feel real good.

Bella wasn't the only thing he was going to miss in American Flat, Utah. He had really enjoyed that circle of toe-toasters who all fought and connived for a select spot close to that wonderful little potbellied stove.

He just wished he were back there right now.

FOUR

It had begun to snow almost as soon as he left American Flat and climbed higher into the mountains. Clint had a heavy leather coat lined with sheep's wool, but the wind still cut through to his bones. He turned his collar up, pulled his Stetson down, and pushed on. It was only about fifteen miles to the top of the pass and then he would be able to ride down into the Green River Basin and be out of the Wasatch Mountains for good. Afterward, he'd still have to ride over the northern section of the Rocky Mountains, but he and Duke could face that when the time came.

After four hours of pushing into the wind, he and Duke were ready to find shelter. Orly had given him directions and said there was a small log cabin just on the other side of the summit, and Clint guessed that couldn't be too much farther. With the wind blowing into his face it was hard to see more than fifty feet ahead, and if he missed the cabin, he knew he was going to be in for a long night.

To stop on this mountain without shelter would be asking to die. No, he thought, I will have to keep moving all night unless we find that cabin. Keep moving until I get out of these damned mountains and into the river basin.

The higher they went, the harder it snowed, and Duke was having a difficult time keeping his footing. The snow was icy and blowing almost flat to the ground. Sometimes it would change directions and just swirl through the trees making them shiver.

Clint was miserable. He tried to guess how much farther it was to the summit, and just when he'd about decided he was there, the trail veered sharply around the side of a mountain and Duke was scrambling for his footing along a narrow ledge that dropped sharply down into a deep ravine.

Clint jumped off his horse and almost lost his own footing on the treacherous ice. He had to grab his saddlehorn to keep from skating over the side of the yawning ravine.

He planted his feet down solidly. He could not expect Duke to carry him to safety. The big black gelding had enough trouble just negotiating the ledge on his own.

"Come on, boy; this can't go on too much farther." Clint stepped out in front and slowly began to move forward. Each time he placed a boot down, he tested the footing and then cautiously moved ahead.

"There's no turning back now," he shouted into the wind. "Can't be too far around this damned mountainside."

But it was. Daylight, what little there was of it, was fading very quickly and Clint knew that it would soon be pitch black and he was bound and determined he would not be on this exposed mountainside. He and Duke had traveled some long, hard trails together, but this had to be one of the worst they'd ever been on. He'd probably not left American Flat more than six hours ago, yet it seemed like days. If he ever thawed out . . .

Duke stopped dead in his tracks, his ears flicked down toward the ravine, and he snorted with alarm.

"What is it, boy?" Clint peered into the ravine. It was a sharp drop, and hundreds of feet below there was what appeared to be a stream littered with boulders and heavy brush all mantled with fresh snow.

He tugged on the horse. "Come on, Duke. This is no time

for sightseeing. We've got to find some shelter. That damn cabin can't be too much farther.''

But the horse wasn't ready to move ahead. Clint never forced Duke. He'd learned from experience to pay attention to the gelding—that if the animal saw or sensed danger, then Clint had damn well better take heed.

''What is it?'' Clint shielded his eyes from the blowing snow and crouched down on his heels. He stared ahead at the trail, trying to figure out what Duke was balking at. The trail looked difficult but no more so than what they'd already passed. And there was no danger of an avalanche, not enough snow had yet fallen even up here close to ten thousand feet. Then what the hell was wrong?

Duke gave him the answer by craning his head down toward the bottom of the ravine and snorting with alarm.

''All right,'' Clint said, ''what's down there that I can't see? Couldn't be a grizzly bear, they're hibernating. And . . .''

The words he'd been about to speak froze on his lips because, ever so faintly through the blowing snow, he saw movement. And then, a snow-covered mound that he'd mistaken for a rock or a rotting tree moved.

''It's a horse!''

Clint strained to see better. Where there was a horse, there was bound to be a rider. But he couldn't see one. There was a chance that the rider could be pinned under the animal, or maybe he'd kicked out of his stirrups and rolled down farther. It was even possible that he'd somehow managed to climb back up to this trail and struggle down into the Green River Basin to shelter.

I have to make sure, Clint thought. I can't take the chance that there's a man down there and he's still alive. If I leave now, I'll always wonder.

Clint tied an end of his rope around his saddlehorn and

threw the rest over the edge. Going down was going to be the easy part; coming back was going to be another story entirely.

"You stand here," he said. "But you may have to pull me up if I get into trouble."

Duke's magnificent head bobbed. The horse understood. This would not be the first time he'd used his great strength to pull Clint out of some mess.

He took the rope in both hands and started over the side. The wind, if anything, had picked up and it was all Clint could do to keep from being blown off his feet. The fallen horse was still beyond the reach of his rope. Clint had no choice but to continue down.

When he reached the end of the rope, he let go and immediately began to slip and slide. His boots got tangled in some brush and he fell and rolled. If it hadn't been for the horse blocking his path, he might have kept on tumbling all the way to the bottom and crashed through the frozen stream.

Clint grabbed the stirrup of the fallen beast and hung on, trying hard to clear his head. He'd taken some pretty hard thumps and he was covered with snow. Freezing to death down here seemed like a very distinct possibility.

The horse was in bad shape. It thrashed helplessly and Clint managed to crawl up and around the poor beast. One of its legs was broken and the other cut very deeply. It was so cold the wound had hardly bled. Clint shook his head and reluctantly drew his gun.

The horse was a fine, chestnut animal and that was one of Clint's favorite colors. "I am damn sorry to do this," he said, "but even if we were in town, you'd have to be put to death. Those legs would never hold your weight again."

The pistol bucked twice in his hand and the horse groaned and died. Clint heard the howl of a wolf somewhere close, but he could not see it through the falling snow. Even if he didn't find the rider, he was glad now that he'd come down to put the horse out of its misery. Where there was one wolf, there'd be more, and he did not like a good horse being eaten alive.

Clint holstered his gun and pulled back on his heavy gloves but not before he managed to untie the rope from the saddle. Underneath the dead horse there was a Winchester .73 rifle, but it was pinned by the weight and Clint had enough to worry about just getting himself back out of the ravine without carrying anything.

He looked down toward the stream, eyes covering every square inch of the steep ravine in search of a snow-covered body. He was just about to decide that there was none when he heard a faint call for help.

"Hello!" Clint shouted into the wind.

An arm raised, flagged helplessly. Clint tied the second rope to the saddlehorn of the dead horse and threw it toward the fallen man. The rope fell way short. But that didn't matter. A man was down and he was in trouble. In this weather, he'd freeze in a few more hours, even if he survived whatever injuries he might have suffered in the fall.

For the second time in only a few minutes, Clint gripped the rope and started deeper into the ravine. When he reached the end of the rope, he sat down and began to sled, digging his heels into the snow and fighting to keep his speed under control. He went that way for almost fifty yards before he came to the snow-covered man.

"Are you all right?" he shouted.

The man was in his early twenties. His face was all battered and scratched and his lips were turning blue. Clint recognized all the signs of a man freezing to death. He had to get this fella out of the ravine and to a warm fire in a hurry.

"Can you move?"

The young man's lips opened slowly, but no words came out. He tried to push himself up on one elbow but hadn't the strength.

Clint stared up past the dead horse to the ledge where Duke was waiting. It was so far he couldn't even see the animal, yet he knew that he'd be there.

That's fine, Clint thought bleakly, now all I've got to do is reach him and get this man out alive. It seemed an impossibility.

FIVE

Clint pulled the man into a sitting position, took a handful of snow, and rubbed his face hard with it until the skin began to show some color. "Come on, wake up or you're finished," he grunted, lifting the man to his feet.

"Can you stand on your own?"

The cowboy was having a hard time keeping his eyes open. He'd been very nearly asleep and that was a dangerous sign. Clint shook him hard and then slapped him across the face, rocking his head with each blow until finally he started to struggle, to make a show of fighting back.

"That's enough," he slurred. "Leave a man in peace!"

"Peace, hell," Clint growled. "Wake up! We've got to get out of here or freeze to death."

The cowboy was finally beginning to understand. His head rolled almost drunkenly on his shoulders and he blinked. "Why don't we just follow this damn old canyon on down?" he asked.

"Because my horse is up there and I'm not about to leave him to a pack of hungry wolves. Besides, we go down deeper, we'll never come out alive."

Clint started back up the side of the ravine. He went as fast as he could, but for every three steps he took, he slid back two until he began to dig toeholds in the snow. From that point on, things went faster. The cowboy beneath him was having an awful time, but he was trying.

27

They reached the dead horse and the cowboy got so upset that he shed tears that froze on his cheeks. "Damn these mountains!" he wailed. "This was an Oklahoma pony, never did nothing but run on flat land. Damned old mountains! He just couldn't get the hang of 'em. We was aheadin' on back home. Hate this damned Utah!"

"Come on," Clint said. "I'm sorry about losing your horse, but you can always buy another. But you can't buy new feet or fingers if they get frozen. Frostbite turns to gangrene. You ever see gangrene?"

The cowboy shook his head miserably.

"Well, you don't want to."

"I ain't leaving my outfit down here."

Clint was losing patience. The light was almost gone and it was, if anything, getting even colder, though the wind had died and the snow had stopped falling for the moment to leave a silent, biting chill.

"We can't get it out of here!"

"The hell we can't," the man shouted. He drew a pocketknife and began to cut away the cinch.

Clint watched him for a moment. The stubborn fool wasn't coming without his rig and there was nothing to do but leave him down here to die or help him. Clint had half a mind to leave him. Still, that saddle and the pinned rifle were probably all that he had left in the world now that his horse was dead. Sometimes a man needs things to hang on to when everything in his life seems to be rock bottom.

"Give me your rope and I'll try to carry it up to the end of mine. If I can tie them end to end, we might get a little help from Duke."

"Why didn't he come down?"

"He's my horse," Clint said, roughly taking the cowboy's rope and attacking the slope. He was tired and his feet were almost numb. It was getting so dark in the ravine that he could barely see to put one hand in front of the other. All he knew was that he had to keep moving up, had to fight this damned mountainside every inch of the way until he made it to the top.

He didn't see the rope until he'd been crawling over it for several yards. His breath was coming in big clouds and his knees were aching.

Clint wondered how long he'd been climbing this way and was surprised to see that he'd not come very far at all. He took the two ends of rope and tied them together—an act that wasted a full five minutes because his hands were dead to feeling.

"Come on!" he yelled down into the darkness.

The cowboy didn't answer, but Clint could hear him grunting and trying to haul his saddle stirrup out from under the chestnut. When a horse weighed a thousand pounds, a man would be strained under the most ideal circumstances to move that much weight and pull his saddle and rifle free.

But two men might do it together.

"Damn!" Clint grunted, knowing he had no choice but to help.

In a moment he was beside the cowboy, heaving and tugging, cursing and shoving that dead horse until they finally had everything free.

The cowboy looked at him and grinned sleepily. He was tall and thin with a pale face and white hair. He looked a little drunk, but Clint knew that he was only feeling the numbing effects of the cold.

"Are you ready?"

"Yep. I believe I am, mister. Much obliged for your help."

His grin was now so wide and infectious that Clint's anger vanished. "I'm not sure we can drag ourselves and that saddle and the rest of your outfit back up to the trail."

"You may not be, but I damn sure am."

The cowboy cut his bridle reins free and used one of them to tie his saddle to his belt. "That old saddle was my father's and he . . ."

"You can tell me later," Clint said impatiently. "Don't you realize we're at the top of the Wasatch Mountains and it's almost pitch black and we are in one hell of a mess right now? If we don't get up to the trail and find us some shelter within the next couple of hours, we might just freeze to death!"

The cowboy nodded. "Mister," he drawled, "I'm a man that just awoke from the Big Sleep and I don't figure the Good Lord brought you along just so I'd have company to freeze with."

Clint groaned. How did you reason with someone like this? He guessed you did not. Clint turned around and used the other rein to tie the cowboy's rifle, saddlebags, and bedroll to his own belt. Then, he started up the dangerous slope, thinking about where he'd been last night and again this morning. Bella's warmth seemed very far away, but the mere thought of a woman like that gave him all the more incentive to get out of a place like this.

Without the rope, they wouldn't have had a chance. As it was, they were having a bad time. Clint could feel Duke above and the rope was moving enough to tell him that it was all Duke could handle to keep his footing and balance in addition to supporting the weight of two struggling climbers.

Suddenly, not ten yards below the trail, Clint heard the sharp barking and then growls of wolves. They were closing in on Duke! He could hear them snapping and snarling. The rope began to jerk around in his hands and Clint tried to scramble faster.

He could hear the fight raging just above, feel the very ground shake and clots of snow pelting him as Duke struggled to hold the rope and yet defend himself.

"Hang on!" Clint swore, grabbing for his gun and finding his gloved hands too encumbered to pull it free, much less work the trigger.

Duke squealed in pain and then Clint heard a hollow *thud* as his hooves landed solidly against a wolf's ribs. The wolf's broken body was thrown off the trail and it hit and rolled down into the ravine so near to him that Clint could have grabbed it by the tail.

A second wolf howled in pain, then the howl was cut short, the snarling grew frenzied, and Duke squealed in pain.

My God, Clint thought, clawing his way upward, don't let them drag him down!

He threw his body over the ridge and wolves attacked him. Clint was so bundled up with heavy protective clothing that their fangs did not pierce his flesh. But they were going for his throat and it was only a matter of time before they would break through his guard and rip out his jugular. Somehow he tore his glove free and then he was drawing his gun, firing into the snarling pack. He kept pulling the trigger until his gun was empty and then he got his hands around the cowboy's Winchester and was using it as a club—striking almost blindly at the pack, feeling the impact of the rifle as it smashed through fur to destroy hide and bone.

Clint was still swinging the rifle when the cowboy grabbed his arm and tore his weapon free. And in the dying mountain light, he was shouting, "They're gone, mister. What you and your horse didn't kill are gone!"

He swallowed; then because he was too exhausted to stand, Clint crawled on his hands and knees to his horse. He ran his fingers over the animal's legs and when he held them up, he saw them covered with blood.

Clint choked back a cry and reached up to grab his stirrup. He pulled himself to his feet and then staggered to the horse's head. "Duke," he whispered, "no other horse in this world would have stayed put because of that rope to us. Any other horse would have run. I am going to get you some help. I swear I will before this night is over!''

The cowboy also ran his hands over Duke's legs. ''No hamstring cut, just some pretty deep gashes. Your horse is going to be fine if we can get him doctored up before those bites get infected.''

Clint nodded. ''And where would the nearest doctor be?''

''Down in the Green River Basin—there's a town not more than twenty miles from here. Big enough for a doctor. But there's this cabin just a mile or two up yonder. Might be somebody there to help out.''

Clint shook his head. ''If there isn't, I'll leave you and push on. I'm afraid that if Duke stops moving, he'll stiffen up so badly he won't be able to go any farther.''

''You going to ride this horse twenty miles tonight?''

Clint led the horse forward a few steps. Duke was limping badly. ''Nope,'' he said, ''I'm going to lead him twenty miles before the night is over.''

And that's the way the conversation ended. The cowboy shouldered his saddle and Clint carried the rest of his gear. He wasn't going to add another pound to Duke's load and he wasn't going to stop moving until they found a medical doctor or a veterinarian—whichever came first.

SIX

Clint and the cowboy pushed on for what seemed like hours but was not. It was impossible to tell the time when you were battling through a snowstorm. The wind blew the snowflakes around and sometimes the gusts twisted until the snow was coming from several directions at once. Clint was often not even sure if they were following a trail. He had no choice but to trust the cowboy.

That trust proved out when the man suddenly stopped and Clint looked up to realize they were facing the front door of a cabin. It was half buried in snow and, in this weather, if a man had not known what he was looking for, he could have missed it by twenty feet and frozen to death on this rugged mountainside.

The door was locked but the cowboy pulled a set of keys out of his coat pocket and had it open in a moment. ''Come on in and I'll stoke up a fire and get some coffee and food heated,'' he yelled, moving into the dark interior with a familiarity that told Clint he had recently spent a lot of time here.

He found a lantern and matches while Clint tied Duke close and out of the blowing snow and the biting wind. When Clint stepped inside, he was surprised to see that the cabin was filled with supplies and the walls were lined with bunkbeds. This was no trapper's cabin, but more like what you would expect in a busy lineshack. The shelves were stocked with canned goods and there were enough beds and blankets for at least ten men.

Clint stomped the snow from his boots and stepped farther inside, watching the cowboy tear off his gloves and start building a fire in a rusty tin stove. "You living here?"

The cowboy twisted around. "Naw," he said, shaving some kindling with a pocketknife. "I been here a few times with friends, but now I am just passing through."

Clint figured that didn't make much sense. A man with a key belonged to a place. Still, he had no interest in why this fella might be lying to him. All he wanted to do was to get a little hot coffee into his belly and maybe enough food to keep him moving until he reached that town in the Green River Basin and found Duke a veterinarian to tend to his wounds.

"I can't stay but a minute," he said. "Don't want to take the chance that my horse will stiffen up too much."

"Then bring him on in!"

Clint grinned. "I believe I will." He figured it would do them both good to warm up a little. Besides, in better light, he could see exactly the extent of the bites.

Duke showed no reluctance at all to coming inside. He was limping badly, though, and seeing his legs with all that blood made Clint feel terrible. He and Duke had been through a lot together; the horse was very special.

"That is quite an animal," the cowboy said enviously. "I can see why you want to get right on down to Roaring Springs."

"That's the next town?"

"Yep. The vet's name is Doc Bennett and he's a first-rate veterinarian. He ranches mostly, but he is as good as you'll find, even in a place like Denver."

"I am relieved to hear that." Clint studied the room. "Looks like you have a lot of friends that stay here."

"Looks like," the man said, turning back to the fire,

which had finally begun to strengthen and bite at the wood shavings. In ten minutes, it would be roaring in that tin stove and giving off plenty of heat.

Clint loosened his cinch and squatted down on his heels to study the wounds more closely. Now, in full lamplight, he saw that they were a little worse than he'd first thought. Both front legs were pretty well chewed up below the knee, and on one of the back fetlocks, a wolf had apparently locked on and stripped away meat right down to the bone; hunks of ripped flesh were dangling down over the pastern to the hoof. It looked bad and, if it became infected, it could even prove to be a permanently crippling injury. All in all, Clint sadly concluded, the poor animal was in pretty bad shape.

"Here," the cowboy said, grabbing a tin of hardened grease. "We can work this into it and that will at least keep it clean and maybe even help the healing go a little faster."

They both rubbed the grease into Duke's powerful legs, he on one side and the cowboy, who talked as he worked, on the other. "Damn shame about this happening to such a fine animal. I got some fish hooks somewhere, and if you want, I can find some line and try to sew this fetlock up. Wouldn't be a very good job, and this is too fine an animal for the likes of what I'd do. My advice is that after we finish with this grease, I wrap the legs and then you either push on or wait until morning's first light."

Clint looked up at the man. "I'm sorry about your horse. You got a way with animals."

"Just horses and mules. I grew up on a Missouri farm and I guess I always did want to become a veterinarian."

"Why didn't you?"

"Aw, you know, never had the money. My folks wanted me to, though. I was the only one of six boys that they managed to put through schooling so that I could get into a vet program. But I just couldn't do that, take any more of the family money, I mean. Hell, all the rest of my brothers and sisters were going to work, seemed only right that I should too. Nearly broke my ma's heart—especially when she found out that I passed the admission tests.''

Clint watched the man's hands working against Duke's legs. They were strong but gentle hands and the fingers seemed have a healing way. It was a shame that this young man had to give up on his dream. Clint figured he'd have been a hell of a fine vet, and they were needed almost as badly as doctors.

''Maybe you can still go to school some day,'' he said hopefully. ''Save up your money and go back to Missouri.''

''That's kind of my thinking. It's my dream. I am twenty-two years old and I can't wait much longer.''

He found a clean blanket and tore it into strips. Clint watched him while he wrapped Duke's legs as expertly as any vet might have. ''My name is Clint Adams,'' he said.

''I know,'' the cowboy said very quietly. ''You are better known as the Gunsmith.''

Clint shrugged. ''That's not a title I hold much fondness for,'' he admitted.

''My name is Mike. I owe you my life but I doubt very much that I can ever repay you.''

''Doesn't matter. Out in this country, no one keeps score. We all have to help each other out a little and I figure you'd have done the same for me if I had been the one in trouble.''

Mike finished the wrapping. ''There,'' he said, eyeing his own work critically. ''Those knots will need checking every few miles. They'll get wet in the snow and start to loosen. You get to Roaring Springs, you put him up at the livery and then send right off for Doc Bennett. Tell him I did what I could but figured I'd let him do the sewing.''

He winked and stood up to go make the coffee. ''You tell

the doc that sewing is woman's work and that is why I left it to him. That ought to get a rise out of him."

"You and he sound like you're pretty good friends."

"Sort of friendly rivals. I pick his brain all the time and he picks mine. I learned a lot of Indian medicine when I was a kid and some of it is as good or better than they teach you at the university. The doc is always telling me that if I was a little darker skinned, I could sure get a job as a medicine man with the Shoshoni or the Utes around here."

"What are you doing now?"

Mike looked away quickly. "Same as everyone else, I reckon. Just trying to get through a tough winter."

"I see." Actually, Clint did not see at all. If he had a dream like this young man, and the obvious talent to make it come true, he wouldn't be wasting his time in some cabin; he'd be earning money any way that he could to get into that medical school and become a veterinarian. But then, each man looked at things differently, and Clint had learned early on that free advice is about worth what it costs.

They drank coffee and Mike fried up some frozen beefsteaks that sizzled in the pan and tasted fine. By the time Clint was feeling human again, it was four o'clock in the morning and the wind was still blowing pretty stiff.

"You go out there and you might get turned around and freeze to death," Mike told him. "Wait a couple more hours until daybreak and I'll go with you a few miles. Then, I can point out the best trail down into the Green River Basin."

"It makes sense," Clint decided aloud. "But I'm afraid of Duke stiffening up."

"You go over there and sleep a couple hours. I'll take him for a short walk and then rub him down good. I'll have him ready to go at dawn."

"I can't . . ."

"You saved my life," Mike reminded him. "Least I can

do is to take care of this fine animal a few hours.''

Clint was too weary to argue. He badly needed some sleep and a couple of hours would make a big difference. ''I thank you,'' he said gratefully.

''No problem. I'll wake you at dawn.''

Clint chose a lower bunk and curled up under a pair of heavy wool blankets. It was, he thought while falling asleep, damned nice of Mike to do this for him.

When he awoke, it was full daylight and a weak sun was finally burning its way through a leaden sky. Clint kicked his boots off the bed and they hit the floor as he stood up knuckling sleep from his eyes. He looked around the cabin and felt a chill in the air. He passed the tin stove and it was stone cold. When he opened the door, he looked out at a white wilderness and saw that last night's tracks were completely buried. At least another foot of snow had fallen since he and Mike had staggered half frozen into the cabin.

He cupped his hands to his mouth. ''Mike!'' he shouted. His voice caused snow to drift softly from the pines. ''Mike!''

Clint listened to his voice fade off into the mountains. He felt an iceball forming deep in his gut and he jumped back into the room to grab his Winchester.

Mike was gone and so was Duke. Something was very wrong. Either they had run into serious trouble or Mike was a thief.

Clint levered a shell into his rifle and buttoned his coat to his chin. He grabbed his saddle and threw it over his shoulder. There were faint depressions that told him Mike and his horse had started toward the east—one way or the other, he figured he was going to catch them.

SEVEN

He had pushed on all through the day until he was staggering with fatigue and if he hadn't reached the basin by late afternoon he knew he would not have made it. Clint had two spurs to drive him on: the need to reach a lower and warmer elevation before darkness, and his driving fury at Mike for having stolen his horse after Clint had saved the man's life. He could not understand a man who would be so rotten, yet there were many such men. He should not have accepted the invitation to sleep for a few hours.

It was nearing dusk when he staggered into Roaring Springs, Utah. His saddle and gear felt as though they weighed three hundred pounds and every step he took was agony. Despite his weariness, however, he did not go to a hotel but headed straight for the sheriff's office.

It was closed up tight and Clint swore. He moved down the street, a man so fatigued he could not walk a straight line. When he came to a saddle shop that was still open for business, Clint stepped inside, dropped his own saddle on the floor, and said, "I am looking for the sheriff. Can you tell me where I can find him?"

"Might try the Silver Fork Café. He is generally eating his supper about this time of day. Anything wrong?"

Clint picked up his saddle. Having been a sheriff himself for many years, he knew the danger of gossip and how a lawman always liked to be the first one to learn of a thief.

"Not so you'd be interested."

As he left the shop, the man yelled, "Hey, give you twenty dollars for that saddle!"

"Not for sale."

"Twenty-five and that's the top."

Clint looked back and shook his head. "Still not for sale."

"Then why'd you haul it in here? Damn showoff!"

Clint ignored him. He had a fine saddle, one custom-made for him by an old friend who'd carved his name in the back of the cantle. Clint would no more have parted with it than he would have with his gun—or with Duke.

The Silver Fork Café was busy; two waitresses were hustling food to a noisy, friendly crowd of regulars and from what Clint could see of the food, it looked damned good. He was as hungry as a bear in the spring and in just about the same foul mood.

The sheriff was easy enough to spot; he had a big silver star pinned on his shirt and a booming voice that dominated the room. In his early forties, the man was already going bald but had a fine handlebar mustache, which he kept waxed at the tips. The mustache looked like the sweeping horns of a longhorn bull.

Clint dropped his saddle just inside the door and went to the sheriff to introduce himself. It wasn't something he enjoyed, but he always felt that it was better for the sheriff to know right out front that the Gunsmith was in his town and that he had no intention of raising hell. Only now, Clint figured he was going to raise some hell and keep on raising it until Duke was returned to him and that Mike fella was brought to trial.

"Sheriff?"

The man was sitting with two others like him, all looking well fed and well rested. Clint could not help but look down at the big bowls of stew and the platters of cornbread they were working at.

The sheriff looked up at him and his eyes lost their good-natured crinkles at the corners. "Can't you see I'm eatin' my supper? You got a problem, come by the office tomorrow morning about nine and we'll talk it over."

Clint curbed his anger. "I have a problem all right, but it sure won't wait until morning. My horse has been stolen."

The man looked over at the saddle. "What did you do, forget to picket him last night and he wandered off?"

Clint was in no mood for insolence. He slammed his fist down on the table loud enough to make the water glasses spill, and he said, "Now you listen to me, sheriff. I am the Gunsmith. I never told any man to wait to see me until office hours and I'll be damned if I am going to be stalled by some third-rate lawman like you. Now, get the hell off your ass and let's find my horse or I'll raise so much grief in Roaring Springs that you'll wish you'd never laid eyes on me!"

The man almost knocked the table over he was so eager to please. "Yes, sir! Why didn't you tell me who you were in the first place? You never been through here so there was no reason why some of us should have recognized you, Gunsmith. It's an honor! My name is Ben Wilson."

The man was so effusive that Clint could not hang on to his own anger. Everyone in the café was staring at him and he knew that he must look like hell—unshaven, wearing muddy boots, face drawn with fatigue, clothes soiled and smeared with Duke's blood. No wonder he wasn't recognized; he looked more like some down and out cowboy than a famous gunman.

"Listen," he said quietly, "why don't you bring along your bowl of stew and some of that cornbread and you and I can move over to that booth so we can talk in private."

He glanced at the other two men. ''No offense meant.''

''None taken!'' they echoed.

After ten minutes and two full bowls of stew each, Clint had his story told and his stomach filled. ''Is the man familiar to you?''

''Sure! He rode in here this past summer and started doing odd jobs. Worked for the Roaring Springs Bank for quite a while. I know our banker, Mr. William Todd, he thought quite a bit of the young man. I think he could have had a future there, but he was always a lot more interested in helping animals than he was in taking care of people.''

''Well,'' Clint growled, ''he has taken damn good care of my animal!''

''Maybe he just brought it into town and . . .''

Clint rubbed his eyes wearily. ''Duke was badly slashed. He was lame.''

The sheriff scowled. ''My guess is that we'll find your horse over at Doc Bennett's.''

''He was the very next man I was going to hunt up after you. Let's go.''

''Don't suppose you'd allow me the pleasure of buying you a hunk of apple pie?''

Clint didn't need to say a word. The expression on his face said it all. He was dirty, tired, and fresh out of patience. Most of all, he wanted to find Duke and then Mike. Horsethieving was a hanging offense. Too bad, he'd sort of liked that young cowboy.

Dr. Bennett was a tall man with a protruding shelf of brow above deep-set, blue eyes. In his late fifties, he had a quick smile and calm self-assurance. He was, Clint thought, a very likeable and no doubt extremely competent man.

''Sure!'' he said loudly. ''Your horse is out in my barn. Mike and I stitched him up as pretty as you please so that when those cuts heal, you will hardly notice any scarring. Be a shame to mar the looks of so fine an animal. Good thing Mike brought him in right away. I'd told him once that a dog or wolf bite can become infected within eighteen hours if not treated. Guess he just made it. No sign of infection.''

Clint expelled a deep breath of air. So that was it. Mike must have remembered that piece of medical advice last night and decided he had no choice but to rush Duke down the mountain. Still, the man could have written a message.

"Is Mike out with the horse?" Clint asked.

"Funny you should ask. I know that kid pretty well and he would not have left that gelding until you arrived except that a group of horsemen came looking for him. Next thing I know, he is riding double with one of them and heading west. Didn't even come in to say good-bye. Not like that kid. Not at all.''

"Did you recognize the men?"

"Didn't even see them until they were riding off. Too far away. They were in quite a hurry, though. Heading right back up into those mountains you came off of today.''

Clint frowned. "Well, I'm just glad to have my horse back.''

The veterinarian held up his hand. "I'm afraid that you can't use him for a while, Mr. Adams.''

"I have a long trail ahead of me down to Raton.''

"It will have to wait at least a week. After that, we shall see. Go any sooner, you may pull the stitches out.''

"I'll wait however long it takes," Clint said grimly as he wondered what in the deuce he was going to do in Roaring Springs for an entire week.

Even worse, every day that he waited meant that the mountain passes would be harder to cross—deeper in snow and more dangerous. But that could not be helped. Pete Haywood was just going to have to hold on a little longer.

EIGHT

Clint was a man who had learned how to live comfortably in small, western towns. He had traveled so widely that he could tell at a glance which was the best hotel, which the best café, and which saloon poured a respectable brand of whiskey. It took him no time at all to discover these things, and after he was settled in, he took a walk about town to orient himself. When he returned to his hotel, he had the impression that Roaring Springs was a cattle and mining town perched on the eastern flanks of the Wasatch Mountains. Heavy forests ringed the higher edge of town, but on the lower side, it was open grassland sloping clear down to the powerful Green River.

The only drawback that Clint could see to the location here was that it was exposed to the fierce storms and blizzards that came funneling down from the north between the Wasatch and the Rocky Mountains.

Roaring Springs did have a small brothel and when he passed it a pretty girl with red hair and green eyes waved gaily down at him from an upstairs window. Ordinarily he might have at least gone to investigate further, though he was not a man who paid for his pleasures with women. Never had been, never would be.

He did see several other pretty women, but he found he could not get excited. He was too concerned about his horse, Pete Haywood's urgent message, and the weather—in about that order. Another concern he had was carrying almost seven hundred dollars and experience had taught him that a man was a fool to leave that kind of money locked in a hotel room or wadded up to bulge invitingly in his pockets.

The Roaring Springs Bank was an imposing structure located directly across the street from his hotel. In fact, when he looked out his window, he could see that the upstairs rooms consisted of someone's living quarters. Clint had seen a man as a shadow behind drawn curtains and a woman who was a real eyeful. She was a tall blonde, almost willowy yet with all the right curves. On the first day he was in his room, Clint had seen her gazing out the window at the distant and snow-peaked Rocky Mountains. For an instant, their eyes met and he smiled, but the woman had seemed embarrassed and had twisted away to pull the curtains quickly. Clint had not felt rejected in the least; quite obviously, he'd caught her by surprise in an unguarded moment when her face had reflected sadness and longing, almost as if she were some caged animal desperately seeking escape.

Clint had turned back into his own room and then he'd collected his money and gone downstairs.

"Who is that woman who lives up above the bank?" he asked the hotel clerk.

The man wore thick glasses that made him look bug-eyed. In his early sixties, he was a short, nervous fellow who showed the signs of a lifetime of sitting behind a desk with nothing to do but reread old newspapers and whatever magazines and books he could find.

"You don't want to concern yourself about her," he said warily. "Not Mrs. William Todd, you don't!"

"I'm not concerning myself about anyone," Clint said irritably. "I was just curious."

The hotel clerk studied him very carefully as if weighing the chance of some ulterior motive. Just about the time that

Clint was going to reach out and grab him by the collar, the man said, "Mrs. Todd is an exceptionally attractive woman. She comes from Philadelphia, I believe. Yes, that's it. Mr. Todd went back last year and brought her out west to live. Caused quite a stir, of course. Mr. Todd, well . . . he put her right to work in his bank after firing his teller. Harry Jones was a fine man with a family. It wasn't right and there was quite a stink made about it, but Mr. Todd stood his ground, and when Harry found another job, the dust settled. But that was quite a shock. Plus we all expected he would rent his bachelor quarters upstairs and buy his wife a suitable home. There are several very nice ones for sale and he certainly has the money to buy or build anything he chooses."

"What you're telling me is that your bank president is disgustingly stingy, a man who hates to let go of a dollar."

"That's not what I intended to say at all! Still, it was rather surprising when he fired Mr. Jones, his teller, and made Mrs. Todd work in his bank all day. Except for a weekly shipment of gold that comes through town and is held overnight on Thursdays, this is a very slow time of the year. No one is buying or selling land or cattle. It is easy to see why Mr. Todd decided that his wife could handle the teller position and do some of the bookkeeping duties."

Clint shook his head. "I guess that's how people like that accumulate wealth. If I were married to a wife like her . . ." He let the thought ride.

"The whole town is curious to know something about her background, but while she is pleasant, Mrs. Todd won't give us a clue as to her past and neither will her husband."

"Good for the both of them," Clint said. "It is nobody's business but their own."

The clerk frowned. "Curiosity is a virtue, Mr. Adams."

"Maybe, but nosiness is not."

The clerk showed a flash of anger at being rebuked, but he

curbed it and said, "Then why did you ask about her?"

Clint smiled with amusement. The clerk had him cold. "Just curious." He did not intend to tell this man that he had been struck not only by her beauty, but also by her sadness. "That a pretty safe bank across the street?"

"My heavens, yes! Mr. Todd does ship a fair amount of gold bullion out of there and not once has it ever been robbed."

"That does not give me great comfort. Only means that, so far, no one has thought to try."

"If you have money or valuables, I can deposit them in our own safe."

"Is that it chained and padlocked to the wall?" It was nothing but a Wells Fargo strongbox.

"Why, yes."

"No thanks," Clint said, heading for the door. "I'll take my chances with the bank."

Outside, there was a hard, stiff wind blowing down from Wyoming and Clint hurried across the street, studying the overcast skies, wondering if a storm was coming. If it would just hold off another ten or twelve days, then he would be over the Rockies and have an easy trip down to Raton.

He entered the bank and the first thing he saw, and the only thing worth seeing, was the banker's wife. Mrs. Todd was standing behind a teller's window, sorting some papers and making notations of some kind or another. She must have felt the cool air from the door because she looked up suddenly, and when she recognized Clint as the man she had seen just a short time earlier from her upstairs window, she had to force a smile.

"Good afternoon, neighbor," he said, moving to her cage.

"Good afternoon, sir," she answered with stiff formality. "What can I help you with today?"

Clint's smile faded. If the woman wanted to play it all business, that was fine because he had never been one to fawn over any woman, not when there were so many to choose from in this world.

"I'd like to make a deposit."

"How much?" she asked, taking a pencil and selecting a deposit slip.

He liked her perfume, which smelled like honeysuckle in bloom. Up close, he saw that she was probably about twenty-five and that her features were bold and her figure was almost perfect. Her hair was pulled back into a tight bun and he tried to imagine what it would look like if it were untied and let to cascade down upon her shoulders.

"Sir?"

"Huh?"

"The amount of your deposit?"

"Oh. Sorry. I was just admiring the color of your eyes, Mrs. Todd. I don't think I've ever seen prettier or bluer ones."

Her cheeks flushed pink but she did not get flustered as he had imagined she might. Rather she viewed him with new interest. "Your name, please?"

"Clint Adams."

"Occupation?"

"Gunsmith." The pencil poised over the paper.

"Well, I truly am. I just don't happen to have brought my wagon and tools along with me on this trip. Passing through on my way to Denver and then going down to . . ."

"How much money did you intend to deposit?" she asked when a chair scraped and an older man stood up to study them through his glass-enclosed private office.

Clint blinked. The sign on the window said MR. WILLIAM TODD, PRESIDENT. "He is your husband?"

She did not even look up but instead nodded. "Mr.

Adams,'' she said tersely, ''will you please tell me for how much this deposit will be?''

Clint shook his head. The man was old enough to be her father. ''Six hundred and fifty dollars,'' he said quietly as he pulled it out of his wallet and placed it on the counter before her.

She wrote the figure down very carefully on three separate pieces of paper. ''We have a very fine bank here, Mr. Adams, one I can assure you that you may trust to protect your hard-earned savings.''

It dawned on him that she was reciting a little prepared speech.

''Mrs. Todd, you can—''

Before he could finish, her hand flew to her mouth and the blood that had flushed her cheeks drained away as she stared at the doorway.

Clint felt a cold rush of air sweep into the room and then he twisted around.

There were four men, three of them with shotguns leveled right at his belly. They all wore flour sacks over their heads, but Clint could see their eyes through the cut holes. And looking at those eyes, he could tell they meant business. Too late he remembered that today was Thursday and that he'd already seen a heavily armed coach unload what he guessed was gold bullion for overnight safekeeping.

No one had ever robbed the Gunsmith before. But now, as the leader swept past him and scooped up his pile of money, Clint experienced a sense of hopelessness and anger. They were going to get away with it and there was probably not a damned thing he could do to stop them if he intended to keep on breathing.

I should, he thought miserably, have waited to make the damned deposit on Friday. But then, almost at the same time, he felt the old familiar tingle of danger coursing through his veins. Despite the odds, there was always a chance he might turn this situation completely upside down. If the opportunity presented itself, he was going to give it a whirl.

NINE

They slammed the door shut, locked it, and now were pulling the shades to the street closed.

Clint's hand drifted toward his gun, but when one of the men tightened his grip on his shotgun, Clint placed his hands on the countertop in plain sight because he knew it would be suicidal to draw and that a shotgun would not be very selective in its aim; Mrs. Todd would be cut down as well.

One of the bankrobbers pushed through the swinging doors and yelled, "Mr. Todd, you reach for that gun in your top desk drawer and you'll be killed for certain!"

The banker had his drawer half open and was reaching inside, but at the warning, he froze. When he looked up at the hooded man, he said, "How did you . . . Mike! You are Mike Chesley! That's how you know that I have a gun hidden in this drawer."

The hood bowed for a moment. "Just . . . just do as they say, Mr. Todd. I'm sorry about this, but the gold you have in the vault isn't worth dying for."

"You Judas! You . . . betrayer! You'll hang by the neck for this, young man!"

"Maybe, but getting yourself killed isn't going to change things one damn bit. So for once, listen to me, sir, and do as they say, and you and Mrs. Todd will be all right. Same advice for you, Clint. I am sorry I took your horse without remembering to tell you I was bringing him down."

53

Clint shook his head. ''Mike,'' he said quietly, ''you'll never make it to a veterinarian's school after a prison cell.''

''This is my only chance,'' he grated. ''By the time I'd have saved enough . . .''

''Shut up!'' the leader bellowed. ''This is no damn time for conversation. Mike, get him to open the vault or I swear we'll blow his wife's head off!''

Mr. Todd shook his head stubbornly. ''No,'' he choked. ''This money was left here in trust and I won't . . . I can't let anyone take it!''

''Mr. Todd!'' Clint growled, ''don't be a fool! These men aren't kidding. This isn't some—some game they are playing. It's no time to bluff!''

''I'm not bluffing,'' the banker choked. ''And I will not open the vault no matter what happens!''

Mrs. Todd's blue eyes filled with tears that glistened. She raised her head and said, ''You might as well pull the trigger and be done with it; my husband loves his damned gold and money far more than he could ever have loved me.''

Clint took a deep breath and expelled it slowly.

Things were not shaping up very well at all. If the stupid, greedy old man didn't open the vault, things stood a damn good chance of becoming very messy, indeed.

''Wait! I may be able to open it myself,'' Mike said.

''No, you can't!'' the banker hissed. ''I have never given anyone the combination to the vault. And for good reason by the looks of you now. You could have had a position of importance here some day—could have been a respected citizen if you had had the guts to work hard. You were smart enough, and I thought honest, too. Just goes to show—hey, what are you doing!''

''Stand back!'' Mike warned. ''I don't want to hurt you. And as for the position, sure, you'd have done to me just like you did to poor Harry Jones, your chief teller for six years.

You fired him! No, sir, I could see what kind of a man you were and I was too smart to make the same mistake.''

"Damn it!'' the leader roared, "would you quit talking and get to the vault. I'll give you exactly five minutes to open it, and if you can't, this woman is dead.''

"That won't help you get your money,'' Clint said. "I think it would be a big mistake. As it stands right now, you can put down your guns and go to jail for a year or two, but if you kill anyone, you will be hunted down and hanged.''

The man's eyes went wild and his gun blurred through the air to crash against the Gunsmith's head. He tried to avoid it, but suddenly he was on the floor trying to keep from sinking under a blanket of darkness. It felt as if someone had exploded a firecracker in a Halloween pumpkin and that pumpkin was his head.

He was drifting in and out of consciousness, and once, he heard a familiar voice cry, "I think it's going to open!''

Clint made himself be still. He knew that his gun had been taken and he could almost feel the tension as Mike worked frantically at the vault's combination.

"One more minute!''

"Listen, I know I can open this thing! Just one more—I got it!''

Clint heard the banker's anguished cry as the vault door creaked open on heavy, protesting hinges. He looked up to see Mr. Todd throw himself at Mike, and then one of the bankrobbers yanked a knife from his belt and buried it to the hilt in his back. Todd gasped and his wife screamed. But Clint knew that there was nothing he could do, and when the banker reeled around and smashed blindly into a wall, he left a bloody smear before he pitched over and died, gasping and trying to reach for the knife that was still planted deep in his back.

"Jesus Christ!'' Mike swore. "You promised me that no

one would get hurt! You said—''

''Shut up. Let's get the gold and get the hell out of here! We're taking the woman hostage.''

''You can't do this. We had a deal!''

Clint saw the rifle swing on Mike and then saw it crash against the side of his face, knocking him to his knees.

''You are with us or against us,'' the man rumbled, leveling the shotgun down at him. ''Tell me right now, which is it to be?''

''I'm with you,'' Mike said.

''Then get on your feet and get to work before someone comes barging in the door.''

Clint lowered his head and pretended to be unconscious. He wondered if anyone was watching him, and when he moved slightly, he saw that the one who still held Mrs. Todd had his rifle trained on him though his attention was absorbed by the exertions of his companions who were rapidly emptying the vault and putting the gold into their hoods.

''Let's go!''

Clint closed his eyes. If he could find a gun quick enough once they were outside, he might very well be able to kill one or two of them before they could escape.

''What about him!''

''Kill him. He's a witness.''

''But you can't!''

''He saw and recognized you, Mike! You're the one who stands to swing!''

''Then I'll do it. Go on and get to the horses. I'll catch up.''

''Use a knife. Pull mine out of the old man's back and do it quiet or you'll have the whole town down on your back.''

''I . . . I will.''

''Mike?''

''No tricks. Be smart. You did your job and you'll be paid.

Besides, we'll keep the woman until you show and we are far away. You be smart and she lives; try anything funny, and she will join the old man in the cemetery. You understand?''

"Yeah. Get the hell out of here!''

A few moments later Clint heard the sound of running horses and then scattered gunfire. So, the gang had been spotted and it must have been very obvious that something was wrong—Mrs. Todd would not have gone on a pleasure ride with three rough-looking strangers.

Clint shook his head and looked up at Mike expecting to see him with a bloody knife in his hand. Instead, the young man was sitting close by on the floor with his elbows on his knees and tears running down his cheeks. He was rocking back and forth, overcome with grief.

"Hey,'' Clint said groggily, ''you were supposed to kill me.''

Mike reached into his back pocket, took out a handkerchief, and blew his nose. ''I want you to kill me,'' he said, tossing his gun to Clint. ''Better you do it quick and neat than I go through the agony of waiting to face the gallows for the death of Mr. Todd.''

Clint sat up. He could hear shouts from the street and the pounding of men's feet on the boardwalk—now, the hammering of fists on the bank door, which had relocked.

"Listen,'' Clint groaned, ''you tried to stop it. I'll testify to that.''

"They'll want to hang me anyway.''

He was right. Clint took a deep breath. ''Tell you what, let's just tell everyone that you were in here on business just like I was and got caught and robbed, too.''

Mike's head snapped up. ''You mean . . .''

"I mean that you're the only one who knows where they are going, even though I have a strong hunch it is to that cabin. And you are the only one who can help me save the woman. After that . . . well, we can just see what happens. I am offering you a chance to right a wrong.''

Mike almost threw himself at Clint in gratitude. ''I'll do anything to make up for this!'' he cried. ''Anything!''

The men outside began to shoot the doorlock to pieces. Clint staggered to his feet. His head was bleeding and Mike had an ugly welt across his jaw so their story would hold.

''What you need to do,'' Clint said, holstering the gun, ''is to just keep quiet and let me do the talking. They'll form a posse and go busting out of here ready to shoot anything that moves. We will not join that posse. But we will find and free Mrs. Todd. Are you game?''

''Watch me,'' Mike vowed. ''You won't be sorry.''

Clint nodded. The door burst open and a pack of men with drawn guns surged inside. But Clint was looking at Mike. He liked this kid; he was very glad he had decided to give him one more chance.

TEN

Sheriff Ben Wilson was not the kind of a man who enjoyed action. He was too heavy and too lazy to bother with small things and, whenever possible, he allowed matters to run their course. But a bank robbery and a kidnapping in his town could not be ignored—not if he hoped to be reelected to a nice, easy job that paid a man mostly for settling an occasional squabble or catching a truant boy gone fishing. So now, with anyone who was anyone in this town standing behind him, he was determined to make a good show of his authority.

"Freeze!" Ben Wilson yelled as he plowed into the bank with his gun up and leveled.

The Gunsmith gave him a disgusted look and said, "Sheriff, you had better form a posse and get after that bunch. They took Mrs. Todd and all the gold."

The sheriff rushed into the empty vault, then reappeared a moment later. "You're right!" he said, turning to face the mob. "Men, they got the lady and the gold. I want every man who can ride and shoot to mount up and come with me. With luck, we can run them down before nightfall and be back in time for supper. Now, come on!"

On his way out, he turned and said, "Gunsmith, I'd appreciate your help. You, too, Mike!"

"I'm afraid we both had better see the doctor," Clint said, fingering his scalp. "We both got slugged pretty hard."

"I'd thought you'd have used that famous shooting iron of

yours to settle the matter,'' the sheriff said with a hint of reproach.

''Might have,'' Clint drawled, ''but something important got in the way.''

''Such as?''

''Mrs. Todd.''

The sheriff blinked with embarrassment. ''Yes,'' he stammered, ''exactly. And you can be sure that her safety will be foremost in our minds.''

''I just hope that you explain that to them,'' he said, indicating the restive and heavily armed crowd of men who had spilled through the doorway.

''We'd wait a few minutes for you,'' the sheriff offered, anxious and almost pleading.

''No, I'm sure you will do fine,'' Clint said, watching them as they scattered to their horses. In all his years of being a lawman, the Gunsmith could count on the fingers of one hand the number of times he had been forced to use a posse. And when he had, it had been elite, a small, hand-picked few whom he felt he could trust to obey his orders to the letter. They were nothing at all like this bunch whose lusting for excitement and revenge was sure to cause more trouble than they were worth.

''None of us is much good at tracking. You didn't hear them say where they were headed, did you?''

''South,'' Mike blurted. ''I think I overheard one say they would follow the river south and keep to the water as much as they could to cover their tracks.''

''Thanks, Mike!''

''Think nothing of it, sheriff. And good luck.''

When they were gone, Clint shook his head. ''When he learns that the gang rode west back into the mountains, you are in for trouble.''

''I know, but you saw that bunch. Bill Dudley and his

brothers would ambush them and it would be a slaughter.''

"Was Bill the one who shot the banker?''

"Yeah. He is a killer, for sure. I was a fool to believe him when he said no one would be hurt. They will be waiting for me up at the cabin.''

"Then, let's not disappoint them,'' Clint said, heading for the door.

Mike followed right after. "Where are we going to get some horses?''

"That,'' Clint said decisively, "is the least of our problems. I can rent''—hell, he thought, those bankrobbers about cleaned me out. "Let's go see Doc Bennett. He'll lend us a couple.''

"Good idea,'' Mike said as they hurried down the street. "I just want you to know that Bill Dudley and his brothers are tough customers. They aren't stupid and I don't think they trust me. My guess is they'll be ready for anything. It's also possible that they won't even be at the cabin waiting.''

"I thought about that,'' Clint said. "After all, other than the fact that they'd want to kill you because you are the only witness, there's no reason to wait and split up the gold.''

"That's why they'd wait for me?'' Mike asked.

"Can't think of one other good reason,'' Clint said. "They figure that you killed me to protect yourself. That leaves you and Mrs. Todd as the only outsiders.''

"You mean you think they intend to shoot Mrs. Todd?'' Mike's voice was strained with disbelief.

"I do. You said yourself that they were killers. They proved it by knifing poor Mr. Todd. That was as cold-blooded a murder as I've seen in a long time.''

Clint shook his head. "If they are still at the cabin, it's just to kill you before they clear out of this part of the country.''

"So I'm the bait,'' Mike concluded glumly.

"Yep. I'll be honest and say that your life will be in great danger when we find them. It will take daring, luck, and a first-rate plan to keep you alive and to free Mrs. Todd.''

''What kind of a plan?''

Clint shook his head. ''I haven't the least idea,'' he admitted. ''And lately, I haven't been very lucky, either.''

Mike groaned but Clint had little sympathy to spare for him. He'd gotten into this with his eyes wide open. Mrs. Todd, on the other hand, had not.

She was an innocent victim, and though her words inside the bank had revealed that she had not been in love with her husband, or had been loved by him, she was still a woman alone in the world.

Clint walked even faster. It would be nice to rescue such a woman as that—perhaps she might even show a little gratitude.

ELEVEN

They had little difficulty picking up the trail of the Dudley Gang once they got up into the mountains where the outlaws had figured they'd given any posse the slip by riding up streams and across steep, rocky landslides that were treacherous enough to make it necessary to lead horses across.

But up in the mountains, the trail was easy to follow and the earth soft and easily scarred by hooves.

The weather had turned foul again, and Clint had turned his collar up to try to thwart the icy blast, but his effort was futile. By the time they had climbed two thousand feet above Roaring Springs, they found themselves in the grip of another snowstorm, one that obliterated the sky.

Clint almost welcomed the storm because it meant that an ambush was unlikely. No matter how sharp-eyed a lawman, it was impossible to see an ambusher in heavy forest before he had time to get off at least one good and likely fatal shot. Clint had lost a lot of good professional friends that way, men with years of experience who had finally been forced to track into heavy forest despite their better judgment.

He did not need to be led, for he remembered well that awful night only a few days past when he had staggered through the snow and almost frozen to death in an attempt to get down to the Green River Basin. It seemed like a long, long time since he had sat near the potbellied stove in American Flat and with nothing better to concern himself with than how to keep his seat near the fire from being snatched by someone else the moment he decided he needed some fresh air or a little loving from Bella. In fact, it had been less than a week.

Pete Haywood, he thought, tugging his Stetson down low over his eyes and trying to peer through the sheet of driving snow, you had better be in some real serious trouble, or when I arrive, I'll make some for you!

They stopped about a half mile from the cabin and tied their horses out of the wind in some heavy thickets.

"You come up with a plan yet?" Mike asked anxiously.

"The only thing I can think of is that you'll have to go in alone and then try to get Mrs. Todd near the door. When you do, throw it open and get the hell out fast. I'll be right outside, waiting."

Mike was not impressed with the plan. "If they intend to kill me," he argued, "then I'll just be shot the minute I walk inside. I won't have a chance to do anything!"

"Look at it this way," Clint said quietly, "right after that bank robbery, you asked me to go ahead and shoot you because you figured your life was over anyway. At least now you have a fighting chance."

"That is a good way of looking at it," Mike conceded, "but you'll excuse me if I don't take great comfort in it."

"Comfort or not, you owe Mrs. Todd her chance."

Mike nodded. "You are right. Wish me luck, Gunsmith. I just wish it were you and not me going in there."

"Just don't panic and try to shoot your way free," Clint said. "Get out fast and I'll whittle the odds down to size."

Mike trudged through the snow toward the cabin. The bankrobbers had made no attempt whatsoever to hide their presence; their horses were still saddled and it looked as if

they did not intend to remain for more than as long as it took
for Mike to rejoin them.

Clint waited until Mike was about fifty yards ahead; then
he checked his gun and started after the man, wondering if he
should have taken his Winchester and deciding against it.
When Mike and the woman came flying out that cabin door,
it was a sure bet that Bill Dudley and his brothers would be
right behind and that meant that the shooting would have to
be fast and straight. Clint had always felt more comfortable
with a Colt bucking in his fist than with a rifle. He could get
off five pistol shots in the same amount of time he could
unleash two with a rifle.

Clint veered off so that he was not in a direct line with the
front door. He saw Mike hesitate, then bang on the door, and
go inside. It shut with a muffled bang and Clint held his
breath, halfway expecting a sudden burst of gunfire that
could only mean that their gamble had failed.

But there was no gunfire. Clint expelled his breath and
shoved his gunhand deep into his warm sheepskin-lined
pocket. Expecting gunplay, he had removed his gloves, and
without protection, his hand would quickly have become
numb with the cold.

He did not have long to wait. Suddenly, the door crashed
open and Mrs. Todd was hurled out into the snow. Clint's
hand came out of his pocket and it came up with his gun just
as Mike appeared framed in the doorway. A gun fired and
Mike staggered backward to crash over and hit the snow, then
roll leaving a crimson stain where he had fallen.

Clint jumped in between the pair and the doorway, and
then he opened fire. His gunshots were muted, low and flat
under the falling snow, but his bullets found their mark and
the cries of the dying men could plainly be heard. Clint dived
through the doorway, knowing he had hit two men but not a

third. When he struck the floor, he rolled and came up with two more bullets still in his chamber, his finger squeezing his trigger.

The room was silent except for the dying gasps of one of the men he had shot. Clint surveyed every crack of the cabin, and when he was absolutely certain that no one was hiding in wait, he holstered his gun and pushed himself to his feet.

Outside, Mike was writhing in the snow with a bullet in his shoulder and Mrs. Todd was desperately trying to unbutton his coat so that she could at least try to stop the bleeding.

"Let me help you," he said, pinning Mike with his knee and then grabbing him by the collar. "Mike, it's going to be all right. I can tell just by looking at the bullet hole and the angle of it that it has missed your lungs!"

He looked up at the woman. "There were only two. Where's the—"

Before he could finish the question, a rifle *thump-wacked* low and hard across the snowy front yard, and its bullet plowed into the cabin, missing Clint's head by less than an inch.

Clint grabbed the woman and pulled her down in the snow, even as his eyes desperately searched the border of forest for the rifleman.

A second bullet screamed in and it tore the Gunsmith's Stetson from his head and sent it spinning. But now, Clint had a moving shadow to fire at and he was determined that he would make both of the bullets in his gun count.

He fired and, to most men it would have seemed like a quick shot, but for him it was slow and deliberate. He heard a yelp of pain, but the shadow kept moving and Clint knew that he had only winged the man.

The snow swirled and he lost his target, and when the snow cleared and he could see again, the rifleman had vanished.

Clint jumped to his feet, reloading his pistol as he ran.

When he burst through the trees, he saw a thin trail of spilled blood and it led him right to where their horses had been tied in the thickets. Only now the horses were gone.

"Damn it!" Clint raged, staring into the blinding snow. He thought of going back to the cabin and using one of the bankrobber's own horses to give chase, but he discarded the idea.

Mike's wound would not be too serious if they could get the bleeding to stop and keep him from going into shock. Clint knew that Mrs. Todd could not do what needed doing all by herself, nor could she be expected to ride down to Roaring Springs and bring help.

It had been their leader, Bill Dudley, who'd been out in the forest and had come upon the battle. Bill Dudley had probably been hunting firewood and had just been lucky enough to have escaped.

Clint shoved his gun back into his holster and hurried back to see what he could do to help Mike. He was sure the gold would still be inside the cabin and, considering that they'd also saved the beautiful Mrs. Todd, he supposed he should feel grateful that things had worked out as well as they had. But he didn't feel grateful. Having no choice but to allow Bill Dudley to escape was like having an itch that he could not scratch. Clint was a man who liked to finish what he started, and as long as Dudley was free, there was a loose end to this affair that he did not appreciate.

Well, he thought, I will get Mike to a doctor and then be on my way as soon as Duke can travel. Let the sheriff and his men take care of Dudley. That is what they are in business to do and I have my own business to attend to down in Raton.

I owe Pete Haywood and his son my life; I owe these people nothing more.

TWELVE

Clint threw another log into the stove and then turned to face Mrs. Todd. "We got the bleeding stopped and I think he'll rest easy for a while. I'd best head down to town and see if I can scare up a doctor who will come up here in a blizzard," he said.

She looked up at him. She had dark circles under her eyes and her hair was scraggly and unwashed, yet she was still so damned good-looking that Clint had a hard time keeping his mind off her. He had to remind himself time and time again that she was a widow whose husband had been shot less than twelve hours ago and still needed to be buried. The problem was that Kathy Todd didn't look like a widow in mourning, not at all she didn't. And, if the truth be known, she didn't act like one either.

Once they had gotten Mike inside and stopped his bleeding, she'd been almost giggly. Clint convinced himself that this was just her delayed reaction to the enormous strain she had been under while captive. She had not been abused or trifled with, thank heavens, but he guessed she probably would have been after nightfall.

"I am truly sorry about your husband," Clint said. "It must have been a hard blow to see it happen that way."

She looked directly into his eyes. "Mr. Adams—"

"Clint."

"Very well. Clint. I won't even attempt to deceive the man

to whom I now owe my life and my freedom. Mr. Todd and I were not close. In fact, lately we had grown to dislike one another rather intensely. My husband was a cold fish, Clint, a money-grabbing piker without a shred of mercy or compassion for those less fortunate than himself.''

Clint did not know what to say to that, so he said nothing.

"I was a fool to marry him," she added bitterly.

"I know now that he was a stranger, though I thought I understood him better than anyone else when we were first wed. I thought that I had made a good deal.''

"Deal?" Clint frowned. "What does that mean?"

"I mean that Mr. Todd and I struck a deal some two years ago. It is all written down and properly notarized—all very legal and binding—thanks be to God. You see, I had always wanted to move out west and yet, being in Philadelphia, I knew no one out here whom I could properly appeal to for help and to serve as a respectable chaperone.''

"Ma'am," Clint said, "you'll have to excuse me, but I am not following this very well at all. Are you saying you married him for . . .'' Clint let it dangle, for he did not want to risk insulting this woman by mistake.

"For his money. Yes," she said almost with defiance, "that is exactly why I married him. He was a well-to-do man, Mr. Adams. He showed me precisely what he was worth at the time and it was well in excess of eighty thousand dollars.''

Clint whistled. Maybe for a big city banker that was small potatoes, but for a man who made it all in a little town like Roaring Springs, that was quite a figure.

"I know," she said. "I was amazed myself. I demanded proof and he gave it to me. That figure is cash, sir. The bank and its physical structure are easily worth another twenty or twenty-five thousand. My husband was a man who knew how to make and keep his money.''

She took a deep and ragged breath. "He was also dying."

"What!"

"That is correct. He had a serious heart condition. That is why he came to Philadelphia, to consult with our finest surgeons. He was devastated when they unanimously agreed that nothing could be done to save him from an early death. I happened to work for one of those doctors and that is how we became acquainted. When he learned that I had always wanted to go out west, he offered the deal."

"His accumulated wealth in return for your hand?"

"Yes." For the first time since the conversation began, she looked a little uncomfortable. "I know how cold and calculating it must sound, and I have no defense for it. I wanted to escape Philadelphia and I believed that a woman without means in the west would be at the mercy of ruffians and rogues. What I have seen these past two years leads me to believe that I was not mistaken."

She eyed him closely. "Tell me, Clint Adams, are you a gentleman?"

He laughed outright. "I don't rightly know for sure," he finally said. "I am a man of honor, however, and that is good enough to my way of thinking. I do not kick dogs that do not try to bite me, nor do I slap kids or women. I have a few good friends."

"Those things, while commendable, do not qualify you for being a gentleman. Can you be trusted with a lady? Can you keep your word?"

"Mrs. Todd, . . ."

"Kathy," she replied sharply. "I do not ever want to be referred to as Mrs. Todd again."

"Fine." He shrugged. "But I have a good idea that the people in Roaring Springs are going to keep right on thinking of you that way."

"I want to leave that . . . that miserable little town as

soon as I can make the necessary financial arrangements.''

"Don't forget that you also have to bury your husband,'' he said coolly. This woman was as pretty as a summer sunset, but as cold inside as a winter sundown.

"Of course. Clint, I want you to take me to Denver.''

"Not a chance,'' he said quickly. "Like I tried to tell you in the bank this morning, I have a friend down in Raton who needs help and I will be traveling light and fast.''

"I can make it worth your time.''

The way she said it got his blood pumping a little faster.

"You said you wanted Mike to go free. That means you want me to lie to the sheriff about his role in the bank robbery. I could send him to prison.''

Clint stiffened. "Now, why would you want to do a thing like that after he got shot trying to save your life and recover the gold?''

"I wouldn't . . . unless forced.'' She reached out and touched his arm. "Take me and a wagonload of my antiques to Denver and I will play along with your story.''

When Clint started to protest by walking away, she caught his arm and added, "I will also give him five thousand dollars to attend a certified and reputable veterinarian's school, and I will give you the same for whatever purpose you desire.''

Clint stopped and turned. "Why me? Why not hire someone else for the job for a couple of hundred dollars?''

"Because I have seen you in action and I believe that you can get me to Denver safely. Bill Dudley wants me very badly, and now that you have killed his brothers, he will want you even worse. I think you are the only man in this basin who has any chance of killing him. I am paying you to rid the world of such pestilence and free my mind from worrying that someday, sometime, he will show up and have his cruel way with me.''

She took a deep breath. "Believe me, Clint, ten thousand

dollars is a small price for the peace of mind I will have when he comes for us and you kill him.''

Clint shook his head. He had given no thought to the idea that Dudley would actually come after him to avenge the death of his brothers. ''How can you be so certain he'll come? Do you know him *that* well?''

Her eyes dropped, but only for a moment. ''Yes,'' she whispered, ''I knew him *that* well.''

Clint turned away to hide his disgust. Any thoughts he had of making love to this woman were swept away by a sense of revulsion. Kathy Todd was a lovely, calculating bitch who sold herself to the highest bidder and even then welshed on the bargain she'd made with her poor dying husband.

''Keep the fire going,'' he said stiffly. ''I should be back in about ten hours.''

She came to him suddenly and, throwing her arms around his neck, whispered, ''Clint, stay tonight and wait out the storm. Stay with me!''

Her perfume made him almost giddy, and even through his big coat he thought he could feel the heat from her body. But as his arms came up to pull her close, his eyes fell on the thin, still form of Mike—Mike who needed a doctor as quickly as possible and who, if he went along with this deal of hers, would finally be able to realize his life's dream and go to veterinarian school.

Clint pulled back and opened the door. Snow blasted inside and it drove her back toward the stove. ''I'm going right now.''

''Do we have an agreement?''

He took a deep breath and looked at Mike. ''Yeah,'' he said reluctantly, ''we do for a fact.''

Kathy Todd smiled broadly. ''I knew you were a very intelligent man! Watch your trail, Clint. He is out there somewhere.''

Clint nodded. ''You bar the door and keep those windows shuttered until I come back. Hear now?''

''I will. Thanks,'' she said almost shyly. ''Thanks for your concern.''

Clint did not have the heart to tell her that he wasn't thinking of her safety but of Mike's. Hs had a strong hunch that Kathy Todd was more than a match for Bill Dudley all by her lovely self.

THIRTEEN

Clint handed Mike the envelope and looked down at him in the bed. "You're a very lucky young man," he said gravely. "Instead of facing a prison, you are going to have enough money to go to veterinarian school and make your mark in this world. Not many get such a chance. You can thank Mrs. Todd."

Mike looked up at all three of his friends, Dr. Bennett whose bedroom he was recuperating in, Kathy Todd, and the Gunsmith. "I'll never forget this," he said.

"Just get through school and be a good vet. Be a great vet!" Kathy said.

"I'll see that he does," Dr. Bennett promised. "I have already offered Mike a partnership in my practice after he graduates."

Mike was still pale from the loss of blood, but he was able to smile. "Is Sheriff Wilson still mad at us?"

"A little," Clint said. "He can't understand how we just blundered onto that cabin so quickly. I told him it was just blind luck. He said that was bullshit, but he didn't press me and I think he is just secretly relieved that the money was recovered and at least two of the gang are dead. He is scouring the country for Bill Dudley and is predicting he'll have the man climbing the gallows steps in no time at all."

Kathy moved forward a little. "Mike, you and I both know that Bill won't be an easy man to catch or to kill. I hope you intend to keep a gun close at hand and the sooner you can leave this part of the country the better."

"I was thinking the same thing." Mike glanced at the veterinarian whom he much preferred to the town's only doctor. "Doc, how soon can I travel?"

"A week." The veterinarian looked at Clint. "You take it easy on that black gelding. He should be fit as ever once he gets the stiffness out of his legs. Sutures came out nicely and I foresee no problems."

"I owe you a great deal," Clint said.

"You've already paid me well. And having Mike back on the right track is even more important to me. I'm getting too damned old to be riding out in blizzards to pull a calf in the night or sew up some poor half-chewed animal."

Clint shook hands with Mike. "I'll come riding through someday. Until then, good luck!"

And that is the way they left it. Duke was saddled and waiting outside and it sure felt good to be back on that animal again. The black wanted to run, for it had been kept penned in a stall too long, but Clint held it to a walk as he and Kathy rode on back toward town.

"Are you ready to leave?" It didn't seem possible that she could sell or give away everything in just a few days.

"I am," she said with conviction. "There is a Mr. Gardner here who deals in real estate and he has agreed to handle my properties and sell them for a fair and honest price. As for the cash and jewelry, I am shipping it to a bank in Dever by the same stage that carries the gold bullion. It is heavily armed and I'm sure that it will be safe. Just to be certain, I have taken a large insurance policy out on everything."

Clint shook his head. "Sounds like you are ready. I have to say that you look almighty pretty and happy for being widowed just five days ago. I overheard some of the women at the funeral complaining that you weren't even hanging around long enough for the body to get cold.''

With a toss of her head, she snapped, ''That body was already cold a long time ago. Bill Dudley's bullet just took the breath out of it is all. There never was a heart to speak of.''

They rode along in silence for a ways before Clint changed the subject. ''Do you know anyone in Denver?''

''Not a soul.''

''Then why Denver?''

''Because it is the biggest city anywhere around and I have some very valuable antique furniture from Europe that I intend to sell. Back in Philadelphia, I could get what I paid for it, but out west, I'll be lucky to get half. I figure Denver is my best hope. I'd have had to give it away in a town the size of Roaring Springs. These people wouldn't know the difference between a silver collar and cuff box and a snuff box; they have little or no appreciation of real beauty.''

Her words irritated Clint. ''Maybe they don't know anything about European artists or fine woodworking,'' he complained, ''but they do know what they like and what they like is solid and true. Nothing fancy, just things of value that last. Sounds to me, Kathy, that you got a case of the superiorities. You might like the west, but you sure haven't much regard for the people. To me, the people and the country are one and the same.''

''How did you come to that conclusion?'' she asked tersely.

''The land shapes the people. Where the land is hard, you'll find folks tough, almost flinty and tightfisted. You go to where the soil is rich and the winters mild, you'll find just the opposite. Out on the plains where it's lonely, the women sometimes go crazy listening to the wind, but in the towns and cities, they tend to be happier.''

She raised her eyebrows. "You are not what you first seem, Clint."

"How so?"

"I don't know. You're a bit of a philosopher, I think, Even I had heard the stories about you. Gunfighter. Killer of only God knows how many. Listening to that, I had in mind the image of the silent, hate-filled predator, a throwback to a more barbaric time when there were no laws and everything was settled by force."

"Those kind of men are all dead or nearing extinction."

"Aren't there always going to be gunmen?"

"I suppose. It will take years before a man with a fast gun won't have anything to gain by his skills. But the day will come."

"And the west will be tamed," she said almost whimsically. "And the western man will be little different from the man in New York or Boston. They shall all be the same. The wildness will have been rubbed out of them, erased forever."

Clint frowned. "You sound disappointed."

Kathy forced a smile. "As a girl raised in a strict and proper home, I once had the great joy of seeing Buffalo Bill Cody's Wild West Show. I will never forget how thrilled I was by all the gun shooting and the thunder. The cowboys and Indians yelling and firing their weapons. Buffalo and the triumphant bugling of the calvary coming to the rescue. It all made my heart race and my spirits and imagination soar. It was . . . exciting and terribly romantic. I guess I formed an image of the west then that could not possibly have existed. Forgive me if I sound a little disappointed."

"Those things are all out here still."

"They are?" She sounded eager to believe him.

"Sure," Clint argued. "What did you expect to see through the bars of a teller's cage? The buffalo are about to disappear, I won't deny that, but the Indians are still raising hell in certain parts of the country. I don't think the Apache will ever be tamed. And out on the big cattle ranches, things have not changed at all. There are still legendary bronco busters and men who can make a lariat come alive in their hands.''

"I want to see them!" she gushed. "Please, after I sell my things in Denver, take me on to New Mexico. I'll pay you whatever you ask.''

"Hang on to your money, Kathy. You've already paid me well. As for New Mexico, well, we will just have to see about that when the times comes.''

"If we make it . . .''

"What is that supposed to mean?''

She smiled knowingly. "Just that Bill is out there watching us right now. I can feel his eyes on us.''

Clint looked around, his eyes sweeping the land and missing nothing. "Point them out to me," he said, "and I'll put a bullet right between them.''

She took a deep breath and said, "One thing for sure, whatever happens in the days just ahead, it is going to be exciting. It will be like a wild west show!''

Clint just grumbled. The last thing he needed and wanted was excitement. He'd had enough to last a lifetime. And driving a wagon of expensive furniture over the Rocky Mountains at this time of year was going to be a tough proposition under the best of circumstances. If we get caught in a blizzard, I will break up the damned furniture and use it for kindling, he thought darkly. That ought to cause some honest to God excitement!

FOURTEEN

When he saw the big, old wagon piled high with a hand-carved dining room table with six matching chairs, a monstrous piano, a sideboard, a bookcase that would take three men to lift, and a heavy, crushed velour couch along with a complete five-piece solid mahogany suite, Clint was absolutely appalled.

"Good Lord!" he shouted. "You couldn't possibly have packed all that stuff into those rooms above the bank! Kathy, we'll never get all that over the mountains." The wagon itself was squashed down on its springs from the weight.

"I won't leave a stick of it, Clint," she vowed. "The man I bought the wagon from assured me that it would not break down between here and Denver."

"Be reasonable, Kathy. It would take six stout mules to pull that load over the Rockies."

She glared at him. "Very well, then, please find me six stout mules and trade those four horses for whatever you can. We made a deal and by heavens you are sticking to it! You've taken my money; now figure out how you are going to earn it!"

That made Clint angry. And if it weren't for not having the heart to tell Mike to return the lady's money, he'd have walked away from the whole mess to climb on Duke and go away in peace.

But he was stuck, so he went stomping around town until

he found six good mules, and since it was Kathy's money, he hardly even argued over their price.

He tied Duke to the tailgate and they rolled out of Roaring Springs at about two o'clock and not one single person said good-bye to Kathy, which must have hurt her though she was too proud to show it.

They crossed the Green River Basin and then began the gradual ascent into the low hills at the base of the Rockies. The road was well traveled, even at this time of year, and Clint's biggest job was to try to keep out of the deepest ruts.

That night they reached the Colorado River and camped in a grove of cottonwoods. All night long, their naked branches beat together in the cold wind, so they both slept badly. While Clint hitched up the team, Kathy cooked a breakfast that they ate quickly and in silence before they climbed back into the wagon and continued their journey.

Clint had never enjoyed mules. He had a long bullwhip and he could make it pop over their heads, but his heart wasn't in driving a wagon. It was slow and boring, at least now while they were still at the lower elevations. He spent a lot of time looking over his shoulder to make sure that Duke wasn't limping and to check his backtrail for Bill Dudley.

There was one moment, that second day, when he did see a horse and rider, but they were far, far to the south, and since this was a frequently traveled road, a man could expect to see others.

By the end of the second day, they passed through the bustling town of Grand Junction, Colorado, which derived its name from its location at the confluence of the mighty Colorado and Gunnison Rivers. They stopped just an hour for supplies and to have one of the mules reshod before it went lame. Then, pushing eastward and ever higher, they continued until just before sunset.

"I don't like the looks of the sky up ahead at all," Clint

said uneasily. ''Those dark thunderheads smell of heavy snow and they seem to be moving straight in our direction.''

''I think they are going south,'' Kathy said, pulling their heavy bedrolls off the wagon while Clint unhitched the mules and hobbled them in a small mountain meadow.

Clint had no intention of arguing with the woman. He knew one hell of a lot more about mountain weather than she did and he figured they were in for some snow this night. The only question was, how much? If they were lucky, this could be one of those early winter storms that dumped a foot or two of snow on the ground and then passed on. By noon, the snow would melt, and though the road would be muddy and harder for the mules, they could keep going.

He gathered two big armfuls of firewood and went out for a third. This night they would need a good, hot fire in order to stay warm. Each time he passed the overburdened wagon, he glanced at the furniture, which she had covered with a new oilskin tarp. Dry wood, he thought, nice to have in a pinch.

They ate dinner quickly, and even before they were finished, the snow was starting to blow hard.

The storm became so fierce that he could not keep the fire burning and it began to smoke and sizzle. Clint looked into the night and hoped the mules did not freeze because the temperature was dropping like a stone down a water well. He buttoned his big sheepskin coat up to his neck and decided that the best and about the only thing he could do was to climb into his bedroll, which he had enclosed in a heavy waterproof tarp of heavy white ducking.

Kathy did the same and for a good long while Clint wondered if she was as cold as he was and if she was thinking that maybe, just maybe, they ought to get together to keep warm. If she had not been a widow and he had not been working for her, he might have asked. But as it was, he would not. So when the snow stopped falling and the wind whipped the clouds away to reveal a chill slice of moon, Clint stared at it a long time before he was able to fall asleep.

Toward daybreak it began to snow again, so Clint stayed in his blankets and drifted back to sleep. He dreamed of warm, sunny days down in Arizona and over in California, of soft prairie breezes floating across the panhandle of Texas, and of the tepid Gulf of Mexico waters where a man could swim and bake just as much as he pleased.

Kathy was awake when he got up and surveyed the snow-covered landscape. Out in the meadow, the mules were gone and so was Duke. Clint wasn't worried. He had expected them to drift into the trees and stand packed tightly together for warmth and with their butts to the wind.

"I'll return shortly," he said, his breath making huge clouds of steam.

Kathy's head popped out of her bedroll and she nodded. "Can we go on?"

"I think so," he told her, "but from the look of things, it could start snowing again any damn minute."

As it turned out, he was right. Before he'd crunched across the snowy meadow, the storm pounded their mountainside once again. Groping far into the trees and calling for Duke and the mules, Clint was beginning to wonder if he would ever get over these damn Rockies and down into the sunshine of New Mexico.

Raton, New Mexico, had never seemed farther away.

FIFTEEN

The wind was ferocious, hard, and driving snow down from the north with a vengeance. He was across the meadow now, groping in the trees, trying to search for tracks and knowing that they would not be visible.

"Duke!" he shouted, cupping his hands to his mouth and yelling into the raging snowstorm. "Duke!"

Clint staggered blindly from tree to tree. If his horse had drifted with the hobbled mules, they could be less than a hundred yards away and he'd still never see them in this blizzard.

After what seemed like hours, he almost walked into his horse. Duke was covered with snow and ice, yet he looked wonderful to Clint who quickly bridled him and then mounted. Clint knew full well that mules, though smarter than horses, will follow a horse even in bad weather. Clint expected that the mules were close and it took only a few more minutes before he found them bunched in thickets. He wasted no time in driving them out of their cover and across the meadow.

"We aren't going to make it," he raged as the wind beat at him and the animals. "Not pulling that wagonload of furniture, we aren't!"

Clint had only one idea and that was to retreat to lower ground until the storm abated. After that, he would simply have to tell Kathy that their deal was off. He would help her

find someone else who had the time to drive these mules far
north to circle the Rockies in Wyoming, then loop down to
Denver. Such a circuitous route might take a over a month
and he just did not have the time. He'd never forgive himself
if he arrived too late to help Pete Haywood because he had
freighted a wagonload of antique furniture for a rich widow
willing to pay him five thousand dollars.

It was difficult just trying to determine exactly where their
camp was, and when he finally did see the familiar hump of
the big wagon, Clint reined Duke in that direction.

Hitching the mules and driving them out of here before
they got snowed in was his major concern and he knew that he
would have to work quickly because the snow was deepening
fast.

Clint was so intent on deciding how he could best harness
those mules in a blizzard that he did not see the man who had
just now finished tying and gagging Kathy Todd. Nor did
Clint see Bill Dudley grab his Winchester and drop to one
knee and sight his rifle.

The swirling, cutting snow and ice might have saved his
life because when the bullet seared across the distance that
separated them, a hard gust turned Clint just enough so that
he took the bullet across his chest instead of through the
lungs.

The bullet corkscrewed him half around and with a cry of
pain he grabbed Duke's mane and the big horse began to
lunge and fight its way through the deepening snow that
blanketed the meadow. Clint's chest seemed on fire and he
lost his Stetson as more bullets probed for him through the
storm. He clung to Duke, knowing that he could not defend
himself this time, that he was hit too badly and rapidly losing
blood.

The booming of the rifle seemed far away, muffled and
desperate in its search. Clint hung on with all of his failing

strength. He felt the gelding smash through thickets and snow-mantled brush, felt the big horse dodging among ice-crusted trees. And then, a low limb caught him flush across the forehead and he was flipping into the air and falling.

He slammed into a deep snowdrift and sank. The fire in his chest quickly cooled and he realized he was going to freeze to death—if Bill Dudley didn't find and kill him first.

Clint lay still. He was face down and he managed to cuff away a depression where he could breathe. He could feel numbness starting to attack his hands and feet. The wound across his chest stopped bleeding as his blood moved deeper into the core of his body in a desperate attempt to keep his vital organs alive.

He drifted into a sleep and then awoke as he heard Bill Dudley cursing at Duke and his inability to locate Clint who was now covered by an inch of snow.

It might have ended for him right there in that snowbank if Duke hadn't come back later when the man was gone. The big horse had to lunge through snow up to his flanks to reach its master. But when he did, the black nudged him, gently at first, then with rough insistence as it seemed to feel the life and the heat draining away from its master.

Clint wanted only to be left in peace; he was dreaming again as he had last night of warm places down south, even of Mexico where he had once met a pretty señorita who had known how to . . . "Go away," he groaned, feebly lifting an arm and batting at Duke. "Let me sleep."

But the horse would not leave and it began to paw at the snow, to stomp it down as it continued to push roughly at Clint with its soft muzzle. Finally growing impatient, Duke nipped Clint on the buttocks and he yelped, then rolled over. His face was coated with ice around the eyes and his mouth. He had to scrape it away to see the big dragonlike horse, steam blowing from its nostrils.

Clint shook his head. He reached up and touched the front of his coat and discovered that his blood had frozen his shirt to his body. He was past feeling cold and his benumbed mind told him that he was in grave danger of frostbite.

He grabbed a handful of snow and slowly began to rub it around and around against his face. When the snow began to melt and the flesh began to sting, he knew that he was not going to lose his nose or his lips.

He pushed himself to his feet and his hand automatically fell to the gun at his side. It was packed with snow, and after he worked it clean, he removed his heavy gloves and studied the gun. He carefully wiped away the last residue of snow and then blew on it until the ice melted. Finally, he dried it in his coat pocket.

The famous Colt he wore was ready and he knew that it would now fire again. Clint pushed it into his holster and reached for Duke. He wasn't even going to attempt to mount the horse because he knew that he would pass out if he tried to throw himself on Duke's back.

I will walk, he thought, twining his fingers into Duke's long black mane. Yes, that will get the circulation back into my feet. And by the time I cross the meadow and reach our camp, I ought to be ready to kill Bill Dudley.

And then, I will bust up that damned monster of a bookcase and I will warm my ice-filled veins before I leave this mountain.

SIXTEEN

They were gone!

Bill Dudley had taken the mules and forced Kathy to ride out with him. Clint staggered to the camp and reeled in a full circle. Everything was gone; the bedrolls, their packs of food, his saddle and rifle. Gone! Thank God he had kept his money in his coat pocket. He clenched his teeth and followed the tracks a short distance until he was convinced that his eyes did not deceive him and that Bill Dudley really had continued up the mountain despite the weather.

Only now did Clint realize that it had stopped blowing hard and that the storm seemed to be weakening. Bill Dudley didn't have to worry about pulling a wagonload of furniture. He'd left it and pushed on with their heavy bedrolls and the sure-footed mules. If necessary Dudley could go on until the weather forced him to camp. He could slaughter a mule and eat for a week or more and he had Kathy for pleasure and warmth.

Clint's first impulse was to go after them immediately. But even as he struggled toward the deserted camp and Duke, he knew that only greenhorns pushed themselves beyond their limits. His clothes were wet, his boots soaked, and unless he dried out and warmed up, he could lose his toes. Clint had seen men who had lost toes and fingers to frostbite, known of men who had whacked them off rather than watch gangrene inexorably creep up their arms and legs toward their laboring hearts. He did not want to join their ranks.

His eyes drifted to the wagon. He managed a grim smile and then he started toward it. He would start with the chairs; their fancy embroidered cushions would start his fire very nicely. When the fire became good and hot, it would require heavier pieces, like the dining table and that damned mahogany parlor suite that Kathy had always been so worried about getting scratched. Well, he would see that no one ever worried about it again. And while his clothes were drying, he would wrap himself in the tarp, even use it to rig a small tent shelter.

I will make it, he thought, if the bullet does not still lie in my chest, I will make it!

The storm had not cooperated with his plans. It had intensified, raged on and on so fiercely that nothing could have moved on the mountainside until it had spent its fury. For three days Clint had hugged the big tarpaulin to his body and fed the fire to keep both himself and Duke alive. Then, the storm finally abated and he waited for dawn so that he could climb on Duke and go after Bill Dudley. Clint had not had the strength to unload the wagon and he'd run out of small pieces of furniture, so he'd just lit the whole works and had one of the grandest bonfires ever on this devil of a mountainside. All that remained was a pile of smoking coals and four iron wheel rims. But the fire had kept him from freezing to death through the bitterly cold nights and he had no regrets.

He was famished; he had managed to shoot an owl to keep from starving to death. Duke had pawed at the meadow and found some forage, but not much, and it hurt Clint to see how the animal's ribs now showed through his long winter coat. And so, when first light peeped over the eastern mountaintops, he led Duke to a stump and crawled on to his back. Clint straightened and turned Duke east and higher into the Rockies. It would probably have been smarter to ride back down to Roaring Springs and find Doc Bennett and let him treat the deep wound across his chest, but Clint wasn't willing to do that. He would go on and not stop until he found and killed Bill Dudley.

The weather turned better, and by noon it got above freezing so that the snow became mushy and the footing dangerous. Clint made no attempt to follow the mules' tracks, for they were covered by at least two feet of fresh snow. It didn't matter much. No sensible man would leave the road and wander into the great silent canyons and wild barrancas. Dudley was certain to keep to the main freighting road that was heavily used in good weather by mining companies to bring supplies and ore shipments down out of the mining camps.

That night he reached a mining town by the name of Bonanza, and though its population was just a fraction of what it would be in good weather, there were still a hundred men or more and Clint was grateful to find a livery where he could bring Duke in out of the weather. Hay and grain were the price of beefsteak, but he did not complain.

"You feed him all he'll eat from now until tomorrow morning," he said. "Just don't founder him on the grain."

"No sir!" The man stroked the horse. "He's a bit on the skinny side, all right. Give me a week, I'd have him fattened up real good."

"At your prices, I could buy you out for what my horse would eat!"

The man laughed good-naturedly. "Costs a lot of money to haul hay and grain clear up here at this time of year."

"Just do right by the horse until I come for him in the

morning,'' Clint said. ''Maybe you can tell me if you saw a man and a woman riding mules through here in the last few days.''

''Sure did. I bought and traded for them.''

''You did?''

''Yep. Gave 'em a couple of good horses and they joined a packtrain that was going over the mountains delivering supplies to Central City.''

''Exactly when did it leave?''

''Two days ago this morning. Ought to be there by now. Them muleskinners, they'll go in any weather at all, but they sure get paid well for it. Me, I'd rather make my money a little easier than that.''

Clint nodded grimly. Two days. By tomorrow when he left it would be a three-day headstart. That wasn't good unless Dudley had it in his mind to stick around Central City for a while. And he just might. Kathy had sent most of her cash on the Wells Fargo stage, but Clint was sure that she had kept several thousand dollars on hand for emergencies. A man could have himself a real good time with that kind of money in a high-rolling boomtown like Central City.

Yes, Clint thought as he trudged across the snowy ruts of the street, with any luck Dudley just might still be there.

SEVENTEEN

They had told him that the mountain passes were closed after the last storm and that the packtrain that Dudley and Kathy Todd had hooked up with had probably just made it through before the usual avalanches had hurled themselves down into the river gorges.

The morning before he left, Clint paid the town's only doctor a visit and learned that the wound was not as serious as he'd feared. There had been some muscles torn, but mostly it was blood loss. The doctor had strongly urged Clint to go to bed for a few days and recover, but he refused. That same morning he had the blacksmith shoe Duke with ice cleats, and on the way to Central City, he figured those cleats had saved them both from losing their footing and sliding off the mountain trail.

Central City was just about how he had remembered it, only bigger. It was the site of one of the biggest gold discoveries in the west and had been dubbed the richest square mile on earth. Clint wasn't sure whether that was true, but in its heyday Central City was producing over fifty thousand dollars a week and boasted a population of nearly fifteen thousand. During the Civl War, the surface and placer gold had petered out and population had dwindled, but now Clint could see that new mining techniques had revitalized the town so that it was roaring as much as ever.

As was his custom, Clint went directly to the sheriff, and when he clomped inside, the man came out of his seat in a hurry. "My God," he said, "you're the Gunsmith and you look like you crawled out of a grave!"

Clint just smiled. He knew he looked pale and thin, but he hadn't realized it was that bad. He quickly described Bill Dudley and Kathy and why he was after them.

"Don't think they're here," the sheriff drawled.

"But as you can see, this is a big town and men are coming and going day and night. I'll keep my eyes open, and if I see anyone matching that description, I'll hunt you up."

"Much obliged," Clint said. "But if I don't find them, I'll be pushing on to Denver."

"You say that this Mrs. Todd is his captive?" The sheriff scratched his jaw. "I don't see how a man could keep a captive in a town without her telling someone or starting to scream or something. Just doesn't seem right somehow."

Clint had given the same question some hard thought. The idea had been nibbling at the corner of his mind that maybe, just maybe, Kathy Todd wasn't trying to escape at all. She had practically admitted that she and Dudley had been lovers in Roaring Springs. What if they were again?

He shook his head. If they were, they were. That didn't change Mr. Todd's having been shot to death and Clint's having been ambushed and left to freeze to death.

"Sheriff," he said wearily, "this whole thing doesn't entirely make sense to me either. Mrs. Todd admitted that she hated her husband, but if you are suggesting that his death was planned by her and Bill Dudley, then I think you are barking up the wrong tree."

"Maybe," he said, "but I just wanted to know if the same idea had occurred to you. I see it has."

"I was there during the bank holdup. It wasn't a set job and

Mrs. Todd was in as much danger as I was. They took her as a hostage.''

''What if they'd planned to split the money and run off together? Then you show up and the plan gets blown all to hell. Seems possible to me.''

''I just don't think so,'' he said. ''I've been around my share of rotten men and women, but Kathy isn't one of them. She's a little bit snooty and has some crazy ideas about the west and excitement, but she is not the type to plan the murder of her own husband and the robbery of his bank.''

''Suit yourself, Gunsmith. But if you are wrong and you find them, you might kill Dudley only to discover that the woman has a loaded gun pointed at you.''

Clint turned on his heel and started toward the door with his thoughts in turmoil. ''Just keep your eyes open and let me know if you hear of anything,'' he said irritably.

Outside, he took a deep chestful of cold mountain air and headed for the nearest gambling hall and saloon. It would take the rest of the day just to canvass this town and even then he might miss them if they were holed up somewhere nearby.

The sheriff's suspicions bothered him more than he wanted to admit. If Kathy and this Bill Dudley were in cahoots and had planned the bank robbery and shooting of her husband, then Clint knew that he was looking for two murderers, not just one. He had never sent a woman to the gallows, not in all his days as a lawman, though there had been a few who'd deserved rope justice.

He didn't like the idea of Kathy swinging by the neck. It turned his stomach to think that she might just be guilty as sin.

So it was that as he began to search the halls and the saloons, he was in a dark mood.

● ● ●

"Whaddaya wanna find 'em for? You damn lawman or sumpin'?"

Clint turned away from the bartender he'd been questioning. The man had seemed to recall someone fitting Bill Dudley's description, but now a drunk miner and his two equally drunk friends were butting into the conversation.

"You talking to me?" Clint asked softly.

"I ain't talking to your damn shadow," the miner said scathingly, straightening up from the bartop and balling his fists. "I don't happen to like people who ask a lot of questions about other people. Nosy bastards!"

Clint was not a man who looked for trouble and neither did he enjoy an occasional fight, the truth being that the hand was never intended to be a weapon. When he used his hands against some bruiser's jaw, he stood a very good chance of cracking a knuckle or busting his fist and that could be unhealthy for a man with a gunman's reputation. It had happened before that a gunman had found himself challenged while sporting a swollen hand and then had to back down and be branded a coward or risk drawing and mishandling his weapon. Neither alternative appealed to Clint.

But when a man, even a drunk one among friends, calls you a nosy bastard you don't think about such things as the possibility of cracking a knuckle or getting the hell beat out of you because the odds are three to one.

That's why Clint planted his fist in the miner's filthy mouth and smashed his teeth back into his throat so that he began to choke and his face got purple as he fought for air. The stricken man's two friends were very indecisive. They seemed to waver between trying to help their friend or making Clint pay for the damage he'd inflicted. By the time they decided, Clint was swinging a mug of beer into their faces and wading into them with both fists.

They never really had a chance. He used his hands on their

bodies which, while they were not soft, weren't all bone like their jaws. Clint sent uppercuts into their bellies and had them bent over and reeling for air.

They had not thrown a single punch and now it was over. Clint asked a few more questions of the bartender, slipped him five dollars with instructions that there was a lot more to come if he happened to see Bill Dudley, and then left the saloon as a roomful of hard-drinking miners stared in amazement.

Sometimes, Clint thought as he slammed the doors of yet another saloon open and marched inside, a man just did not want to be trifled with.

EIGHTEEN

It had taken Clint two more hard days of riding out new storms before he dropped down on the western terminus of the Great Plains and the mighty city of Denver. From the vantage of the foothills he could see the shiny tracks of three railroads fanning north, east, and south.

Once just another boomtown, Denver had eclipsed Santa Fe as the major center for commerce between San Francisco and St. Louis. No longer did its fortunes hang so precariously on the discovery and continual flow of gold and silver. Denver boasted a flourishing and well-rounded economy based on ranching, railroading, and trade generated from a growing population.

When Clint saw how big the city had grown, he felt a sense of hopelessness because it would take weeks to search for Bill Dudley and Kathy. He did not have weeks to spare and the thought occurred to him that every day he spent here Dudley might be putting to use outdistancing him on his way to somewhere else.

As he rode down toward the big city, Clint realized that he would have to work smart and work fast or he would lose the trail. He decided that he would begin his search at the Wells Fargo office and determine if Mrs. Todd had collected her cash and jewelry. If so, he could at least rest assured that they had been through Denver and how long ago it had been. Kathy Todd was such a beautiful woman and the sum of money she stood to collect so large, it seemed likely to Clint that she would be remembered.

He rode down Larimer Street and crossed to the Wells Fargo office and patiently waited in line until a harried clerk said, "Next!"

Clint stepped up to the counter and said, "I would like to know if a rather beautiful young woman about five feet nine with blond hair came in to collect a large sum of money and jewelry shipped from Roaring Springs, Utah."

The clerk, a young man with a nervous tick up near his right eye, blinked. "What?"

Clint took a deep breath and repeated the question slowly, all the time aware that the line behind him was growing longer.

"Mister, this isn't an information desk and I haven't the slightest idea what the devil you are talking about! Now, if you don't—"

Whatever else he had been about to say was forgotten as Clint's hand shot across the counter and he grabbed the man by the throat. "Young man," he said, "you better reconsider your way of looking at this. I have been pistol-whipped, shot, and left to freeze in a blizzard, and my saddle, rifle, and bedroll have been stolen by the man who accompanied the woman I just described. So think hard and give me a straight answer or face the consequences!"

He had lifted the man right up on the tips of his toes and put fear into his eyes. "I . . . I don't remember," he choked. "Listen, we see sixty or seventy people a day here! I can't . . ."

"You must keep records of that kind of money! There have to be receipts on file. Where are they?"

"Let go of him," an older man with thick glasses and an air of authority ordered.

"Mr. Arnold, this man just—"

"I saw it. You ignored a civil question and failed to give him a respectful answer. That is not the kind of service that built this company, Phillip!"

"But, sir—"

"Get back to your duties," the manager said tersely. "I will help this gentleman. Come with me to my office."

When they were inside, the man extended his hand. "Cyrus Arnold, Office Manager. It is indeed a pleasure to meet you, Gunsmith!"

Clint relaxed. "Where do you know me from?"

"Cheyenne. You helped our company recover a great deal of money. I never had the chance to extend our thanks; I do so now."

He offered Clint a cigar and waved him into a seat. "Now," he said, "tell me how I can be of service."

Clint explained what he needed and finished by saying, "I thought you might have records. They could not have picked up that package over five days ago."

"Then it will take only a couple of hours to go through the receipts," he said. "Do you want to wait here or come back later?"

"I want to help you."

"Fine! We shall do it together."

Just twenty minutes later they found the signed receipt and Clint sighed with audible relief. It was dated just two days ago, and though he couldn't be sure, the signature looked to be that of a woman's hand. It was signed by a Miss Kathy Ault. He guessed she used her maiden name, which did not surprise Clint because the woman had wanted no reminder of her deceased husband.

"Who initialed this?"

"That would be my assistant, James Terry. He is out on the loading dock. Shall I call him in for a moment?"

"I'd appreciate that."

Moments later, the Wells Fargo ticket agent came inside. "Mr. Arnold has instructed me to help you in any way possible."

He was a man in his late forties, trim, and intelligent looking with a long handlebar mustache just starting to go silver.

"Tell me whatever you can remember about the woman who picked up this package two days ago," Clint said.

He just glanced at it. "Sure. A man doesn't forget a woman like her. She was beautiful. Tall, slender, and in her early to mid-twenties. She had blue eyes and a nice smile. Her hair was long and dark brown."

"Brown! Are you sure?"

"Of course." Terry frowned. "I wouldn't forget a woman that lovely even if I am probably old enough to be her father."

"Was she alone or with a man?"

"Alone, I think. At least I saw no one with her."

"Did she act nervous? Say anything unusual?"

"No. As a matter of fact, she seemed quite relaxed and very jolly. She smiled at everyone and you couldn't help but smile back. I would pay to work here if I had a few like her every day."

It was meant as a joke, but Clint wasn't prepared to give so much as a smile. "Do you have any idea of her plans? Did she say where she might be staying or for how long?"

"No. And we are instructed not to ask any personal questions. It was none of my business. I am curious, however, what business it is of yours."

"That will be all, Mr. Terry," Mr. Arnold said abruptly. "We appreciate your keen powers of observation and now I ask that you redirect them back to the loading dock."

Terry smiled and left.

"Good man," Clint said.

"He'll take my job some day. Was he any help?"

"He was. Problem is, he raised more questions than answers. The woman I seek has blond hair."

"Hair is easily dyed, Gunsmith."

"True," he said. "But would a kidnapped woman act so happy? And why wouldn't she escape if she was alone?"

"Maybe she did. Have you checked with our sheriff's department yet?"

"My next stop."

"You'll find Sheriff Humphrey one of the best. Maybe your woman has already contacted him."

"I hope so," Clint said, but as he thanked Arnold for his cooperation, he was thinking that, somehow, he had the feeling that Kathy Todd or Kathy Ault was not acting at all like a frightened widow.

And as he hurried outside through the crowded Wells Fargo office, he was thinking that something very strange was going on. Either Kathy was one hell of a daring woman, one who thrived on intrigue and danger, or she was dead guilty of conspiracy to murder and rob her husband and his bank.

Either way, things were getting more and more interesting by the minute.

NINETEEN

Clint shrugged. "So that's the whole story. And since I'll be combing this city for both of them, I wanted you to know the reasons. I may have to lean on a few people to get the answers. But you might have a killer and a bank robber here in Denver."

The sheriff was an angular redhead with big hands and freckles. He had to be at least fifty years old. Clint had sensed an immediate competence in the man; he was a veteran lawman and that was the only kind he wanted to work with.

Sheriff Humphrey laced his thick fingers behind his head and leaned back in his chair. "Sounds a little sticky," he said. "You don't know if you're looking for a woman with dark brown or blond hair, and you've never even seen this Bill Dudley fella."

"Like I said, he was wearing a hood when he shot Mr. Todd and robbed the bank. And up in the mountains, it was snowing so hard, I never had a chance to see him before he shot me."

"That gives him a rather significant advantage, wouldn't you say?"

"I would. But it changes nothing. Can you offer me any help?"

"Not much, I'm afraid. My advice would be to check the railroad offices. There are also a couple of daily stages leaving Denver. Gunsmith, I hate to tell you this, but there are a lot of ways that woman could have left town and the odds are that she took one of them. Maybe she went back east where she came from.''

Clint shook his head. "No, that's about the only thing I'm certain of." He stood up. "I better get to looking. Appreciate your help.''

"Keep in touch," the sheriff advised. "I'll pass the word around that you are here working on a case and in full cooperation with this office. Might save me some heat. There are a lot of men who still fear your reputation.''

"Only the ones who have a good reason to," Clint said.

He had taken the sheriff's advice and inquired at all the railroad ticket offices as well as the stages. He had checked all the livery stables and come up empty until he came to the last one at the edge of town. It was a small, out of the way barn, and the man who tended it was cantankerous and more interested in his forge than the horses out back.

"Yeah," he said, working his bellows and turning a horse-shoe over and over until it was a fiery orange, "I bought her horse, and if you have some notion of telling me it was stolen or some such damn thing, then I say get the hell off my property 'cause I got a clean bill of sale.''

"I want to see it.''

"Come back later when I ain't busy.''

The man was big, dirty, and strong and Clint was not interested in seeing who could whip whom. So he just pulled out his gun and stuck it to the blacksmith's ear and said, "I believe you will show it to me now.''

It never ceased to surprise Clint how the barrel of a .45 Colt could change a man's attitude and personality so radically. The chances were ninety-nine out of a hundred that a man with a gun to his head would be cooperative. Once in a while, though, instead of being helpful, the person being persuaded went crazy. Maybe someone, somewhere had pulled a gun on him before and then humiliated him, Clint didn't know or care. What mattered now was that the giant blacksmith was that one in a hundred who was going berserk.

The man reached up and swatted Clint's gun aside just as if it were a fly buzzing his ear. Clint took a backstep. "Now wait a minute," he said, hands up. "I didn't really want to kill you over this. Let's be reasonable men."

In answer, the blacksmith balled his fists, roared with his lips curled back, and charged.

Clint tried to pistol-whip the giant coming in at him but tripped over a box of old horseshoes and went crashing into the dirt. When he looked up, all he saw was boots coming down at his face.

Clint rolled sideways and the man bellowed in anger and frustration as his boots slammed into the earth. He whirled and lashed out with a looping right hand that knocked Clint's Stetson sailing into the water trough.

"Hey, now wait just a damned minute," Clint swore. "That was a good hat you probably ruined. All I want for you to do is to show me that horse and your bill of sale!"

"What I'm going to show you is knuckles and blood— your blood, you nosy son of a bitch!"

Clint stared at the gun in his hand. He had a sinking feeling that about the only way he had a chance of stopping this fellow was to shoot him in the knee. That seemed pretty drastic and yet . . .

The man charged again. Only this time, he was expecting something tricky, and when Clint tried to trip him, he jumped the outstretched leg, threw his big arms around Clint, and drove him into the ground. He was fifty pounds heavier and a damn sight stronger. He got both knees on Clint's chest and then he reared back to punch his head off. Clint palmed his gun and drove it into the man's face—the blacksmith's nose broke with a popping sound. The man howled in pain and reared back, grabbing his bloody nose. Clint kicked his legs up, locked them around the man's head, and jerked him over backward.

They both got up, chests heaving, each circling the other and waiting for an opening. Clint holstered his gun. He wasn't going to shoot this idiot and there was no use trying to bluff any longer. The man was either insane or fearless. Clint feinted a right cross, and when the blacksmith threw up his massive left forearm to block the punch, Clint smashed an uppercut against his jaw and then followed it with a boomer of a right cross.

Both were hard shots, as good as he had in his arsenal, and neither seemed to bother his opponent, who lowered his shaggy head and came in swinging.

Clint blocked two punches, caught a third on the collarbone that spun him halfway around, then drove a fist into the man's belly. It was like punching the butt of a mule—solid, no give at all.

"Stand still and fight!"

Clint shook his head. "I'll take care of business my way, you give it your best try, and we'll see what happens next."

The blacksmith swung a roundhouse punch that would have flattened an ox. Clint just managed to jump back out of range. He felt the air move as the big fist swept past and then he caught the blacksmith half-turned and off balance. He moved in fast and punched him twice in the gut, then drove a fist down against his cheekbone that wobbled the man.

For the first time, Clint saw that the blacksmith was vulnerable. He grabbed him by the belt, and in a moment of inspiration, propelled him face down into the horse-watering trough.

The blacksmith's belly slammed down hard on the edge of

the tank and it must have knocked the wind out of his lungs because he took a deep breath of dirty water and reared back choking for air. There was slime coating his face and Clint swarmed over him, banging away with both fists until the giant crashed down and lifted one big paw in a sign that he was whipped.

That was the best news Clint had heard all day. By rights, he should have had his own clock cleaned, but there are times when a smaller and faster man can win if he uses his head. Besides, the blacksmith must have filled his lungs with water and nobody can fight while drowning.

Clint lowered his fists, and he waited until the blacksmith stopped choking and caught his breath. ''The girl—was she alone or with another man?''

He rolled over in the mud and stared at Clint through half-closed eyes. His big chest was heaving and his lips were already as big and puffed as a couple of sausages. ''Alone,'' he said finally, ''but a man came looking for her yesterday. I didn't like him.''

''That makes two of us,'' Clint said, poking his aching hands into the water trough to keep down the swelling. ''Did he say what he wanted with her?''

''Nope. And I told him nothing. He was in bad shape, though.''

''How?''

''Bum leg. It was all bandaged up. He was limping real bad. Say, mister, next Saturday night some of the best men in Denver are going to stage a fight. I won the right to take on this so-called champion fighter who travels around. He's huge, bigger than me, and they call him Bone Crusher. Maybe you should take my place in the ring. You won the honor just now. Nobody has ever gone three rounds with Bone Crusher. You do, you earn a thousand bucks. Don't even have to whip him, just be standing up at the end. The way you dance and move, I think you could win that prize money.''

"Think again," Clint said, rubbing his bruised knuckles on his shirt. "But I wish you all the luck in the world.''

"Any tips you can give me?''

"Just one.''

"What's that?''

"Don't fight near a water trough.''

The man blinked for a moment and then he burst out laughing as if he had never heard anything so funny in his entire life. "That's good, real good!'' he kept squealing. "Wait until I tell the boys that one!''

Clint relaxed and smiled. "Why don't you show me that horse now, and then I will be on my way.''

"Hell, don't hurry off. I ain't been whipped since I was a little kid. People find out you beat me, that makes you a celebrity in Denver.''

Clint looked around. "Tell you what, why don't we make it our little secret.''

"You mean not tell?'' Obviously, the man could not believe his ears.

"Exactly.''

"But why? You beat me fair and square.''

"Maybe, but let's just say I'm a man who likes to keep quiet.''

The blacksmith rolled and stood up in his size twelve boots and nodded. "Suit yourself," he drawled, pulling out a dirty handkerchief, soaking it with water and then smearing the blood from his nose all over his face. "But it ain't every day a man gets to be a damned celebrity.''

"I guess not,'' Clint said. "Now how about a look at that horse?''

Ten minutes later he was riding Duke back to town with a

new sense of urgency. It seemed pretty clear from the blacksmith's description that the man after Kathy was Bill Dudley and that the pair were not in cahoots.

Had she shot Bill and then escaped? It seemed the only possible answer. And if that were true, maybe she was running away from him and had already left Denver. She might have sold this horse only to buy another in an attempt to throw Dudley off her trail. Maybe that was why she had dyed her blond hair brown.

Clint arrived back at the sheriff's office with even more questions than he had an hour before. He would tell the sheriff about this latest discovery and that they had better find Kathy fast—or Bill Dudley would kill her for sure.

TWENTY

Where do I begin to search for a woman like Kathy?—that was what Clint kept asking himself over and over. Ironically, it might also be the same question that Bill Dudley was asking himself. Clint thought about Kathy and decided that he would try the hotels first, starting with the best ones and then working his way down. Kathy had a lot of money and she would not be slow in spending it, unless Clint missed his guess. She seemed to him like the kind of woman who liked expensive things, expensive things like antiques!

He knew then that if she were in town she would have visited the antique stores. She might even be expecting Clint to make it over the mountain passes and bring her wagonload of furniture into Denver to sell.

The first antique dealer he encountered remembered Kathy very well because she had spent a long time considering a French Provincial settee and a rare Chinese vase. But she did not know where she might be or if she would return to make the purchases.

"If you find her," the distinguished lady said, "tell her she can have both items for the sale price of just eight thousand."

Clint gulped. The settee looked threadbare and the vase was nothing special. "Dollars?"

The shopkeeper frowned. "What else?"

He smiled, jotted down the names of two other antique

113

shops, and left in a hurry. My God, he thought, if that little bit of stuff costs eight thousand, what did her furniture that I burned cost? Maybe, he thought wryly, it would be smarter to avoid Kathy entirely.

But he couldn't, of course. She was being stalked by Dudley and her life was in grave danger.

Clint learned nothing at the next antique store, but then the merchandise looked more like secondhand junk furniture than antiques to him, and he supposed Kathy would have turned her nose up at the collection.

The moment he saw Sanderson's Antiques, he knew this was the place. It was large and classy—definitely the premier antique shop in Denver. Clint took a deep breath and crossed his fingers. If these people couldn't help him, he was right back to square one without a clue as to where to go next.

"Clint! Oh, Clint!" she cried, looking up from the beautifully carved little English writing desk she had been inspecting. "I knew you'd come through!"

She rushed down the aisle and to the surprise of everyone, especially Clint, she threw herself into his arms and happily showered him with kisses. Clint didn't know what to do other than to put his arms around her and return the favor. Her kisses took on a definite hungry nature and he felt himself being stirred by her obvious passion.

As far as he was concerned, he would have liked to continue, but the antique shop was frequented by a bunch of rich old ladies who were clearly appalled by the spectacle.

"My darling!" she whispered, pulling back and looking deep into his eyes. "I was so afraid for you. I . . ." Overcome by emotion, she could not continue, and she wiped her glistening eyes with a silk scarf.

Clint shook his head. "I think we had better get out of here and go somewhere we can talk in private, Kathy. You've got a lot of explaining to do."

"Explaining? What an odd way of putting it, Clint. But first, where is my lovely furniture?"

He took a deep breath. "Come to think of it, maybe we both have some explaining to do."

She took him to her hotel, an elegant two-story palace with great hanging chandeliers. It was exactly the kind of place she would choose; rich, expensive, and filled with shiny old furniture that was probably all antique. The room itself was bigger than the normal log cabin, and it had a big canopied bed, which Kathy sprawled out on to his discomfort, while he chose an overstuffed chair.

"Well," he said, "I think I'll get mine over with first. You know I was shot and left to die in the snow."

"Yes," she said sadly. "I hated that man for doing that to you. I begged him to let me help you until I realized that, if I did, he would kill you for sure."

"Good thinking. Well, anyway, after I got back to camp, I was in pretty rough shape. Half frozen and wet, temperature falling as night came on, and the wind getting strong—and no bedroll!"

"I know," she wailed. "I wanted him to leave one of them, but of course, he would not. He took your saddle and things and there was nothing I could do to stop it. He forced me on to a mule and we rode away."

She patted the bed beside her. "Come over here, Clint. You look tired and you have lost so much weight!"

"I damn near starved to death up there—that and froze." He smiled. "That brings me to the reason I had to . . . well, Kathy, I know how much you valued that antique furniture, but . . ."

"You didn't!" she screeched, her face losing its color. "Clint, you couldn't!"

"Afraid so," he said. "It kept me alive for a couple of

days. Couldn't have made it without it that furniture—burned real nice, solid oak.''

''Ohhh,'' she groaned. ''Do you have any idea what that furniture was worth? Thousands!''

''Like I said, I am sorry, but I have a few questions of my own.''

''Such as?'' Her voice was as chill as the wind off the nearest mountains.

''Such as why you changed the color of your hair and how you managed to escape?''

''I changed my hair color so that it would be hard to recognize me. As for my escape, I just had to wait until the right moment and then I grabbed his gun and shot him.''

''Did you kill him?''

''Yes.''

''No, you didn't,'' Clint argued. ''He's in town looking for you right now.''

It was her second major shock within minutes and, to her credit, she took it better than the news of her furniture. ''Are you sure?'' she asked incredulously.

Clint told her what the liveryman had said. ''So you couldn't have killed him. Just shot him is all.''

Kathy jumped up from the bed. ''I've got to get out of this town!'' she cried. ''He'll kill me!''

Clint grabbed her by the arm. ''Slow down. He is going to try to kill you, but I want to take the man alive. He's got some answers I want.''

''I've told you everything.''

''I hope so,'' Clint said, ''because if I discover that you and he set this whole thing up to get rid of your husband—''

''Clint! You can't—you can't possibly believe that I would . . . you do believe that is what happened!''

She swung at him. He grabbed her wrist and then had to grab the other one to stop her from clawing out his eyes.

"Hold still, damn it! I don't believe anything yet. I just want to talk to Bill Dudley before he swings by the neck."

She relaxed. "You want to use me as bait. Is that it?"

"Yep."

"And if I refuse to play along with this?"

"Then, I will say to hell with it and let Bill Dudley find you and do what he wants."

She took a deep breath and expelled it slowly. "And here I thought you were a real gentleman. Now you tell me I have no choice but to cooperate or you will allow me to be murdered."

Clint shrugged. "It is a hard life out here. You've been sheltered in Roaring Springs. Besides, I'd have thought you'd want the murderer of your husband to face justice as much as I do."

"All right," she said finally. "We will play it your way. But if I get maimed doing this, I'll never forgive you, Clint Adams."

He grinned. "I'll keep that in mind. Now, here's what you are going to do."

TWENTY-ONE

There was nothing complicated in the Gunsmith's plan, nothing at all. It had always been his philosophy to keep things simple and straightforward; that way there was always less chance of something going wrong. What he wanted was for Kathy to be an easy target for Bill Dudley and the easiest way for that to happen was to have her do a lot of shopping and moving around.

That part of it Kathy liked. She loved to spend money and there was no end to the things she would enjoy buying. She had, however, made a few conditions.

"If I am going to spend my money on nice things and be bait for Dudley, then I expect you to take me—and my new things—down to Raton, New Mexico, with you."

"What for?"

"Well," she said, "I have been asking people about that town and they say that it is surely a fine place to live and invest in. Denver real estate is already overpriced, and since I have to do something, I thought I might start my own antique shop in Raton. I've already made inquiries, and there isn't a single one there! I'd be the first and only. Isn't that something?"

"Yeah," he said without enthusiasm. "What a fine idea. But have you forgotten that I am supposed to be there before Christmas?"

"We still have time. Besides, there are no big mountains

to cross between here and there so it will be an easy trip.''

There was some truth in her words. If they left within the week, they should still have an easy trip, even riding in a wagon. Besides, the tone of the letter had contradicted the *urgent* stamped on the envelope. Clint had the feeling he might go all the way down there only to discover that old Pete had just thought it might be nice to have a close friend on hand to celebrate the holiday season in his Hot Lizard Saloon, providing he still owned it.

''Clint, either you agree to take me and a wagon on down, or I'll get on the first train out of Denver and simply run away from Bill. I'm not putting my life on the line for nothing.''

''Nothing? The man murdered your husband and robbed his bank.''

''I've heard that the money was all recovered,'' she said. ''And I am sorry that Mr. Todd was killed, but you were there and you saw as clearly as I did that he died because of his own greed and stupidity. Those men had no intention of killing anyone. But Mr. Todd forced them to do it and for that, you were pistol-whipped and I was kidnapped!''

''You don't run long on sympathy, do you, Kathy?''

''That man lied to me and made my life miserable.''

Her lower lip quivered. ''I know that you think I am cold-hearted; I can't help that. Mr. Todd was a despicable man in every way. I saw him evict poor families from their small farms and ranches for being late on payments; he did the same to people in town. How many people were at his funeral?''

''Three, no four,'' Clint reluctantly admitted.

''That's right, if you count the corpse. Otherwise, it was just you, me, and the mortician. That ought to tell you something about how much Mr. Todd was hated in Roaring Springs.''

He nodded, knowing that he could not argue with her on the point. ''All right, we have a deal.''

''Almost,'' she said, holding up one finger. ''First, I'd like to know how you intend to protect me if he just decides to walk up and open fire.''

Clint rubbed his jaw. Bill Dudley hadn't seen him, but he might have heard that the Gunsmith was on his trail. And if he were seen shadowing Kathy, Dudley might ambush her and escape.

''I'll wear a disguise,'' he said. ''I'll powder my hair white and find someone to apply makeup to my face so that I look old. Then, I'll wear some suspenders and have a walking cane and totter around like an old, old man. I can wear a battered hat and look like a hundred other old men who rode the broncs way too long.''

She pursed her lips. ''All right. I'll apply the makeup and you have to promise to stay very close.''

''I solemnly promise.''

''In that case,'' she said, putting her arms around his neck and kissing him long and passionately, ''I think we ought to seal the bargain.''

Her eyes slipped to the bed and Clint smiled. ''I think that's the best idea I've heard in quite a while.''

Clint watched her undress. She was even more beautifully put together than he had imagined. Her legs were long and perfect; her hips nicely rounded; her belly flat and firm. He cupped her breasts, liking the size and shape of them—not as large as Bella's but plenty big enough for a man to enjoy.

When his tongue played with her nipples, she shivered with hungry urgency and her hands worked to unbutton his shirt, then his pants. A moment later, her hands were groping for his manhood.

He felt her take him and then his pants were dropping and

she was kissing his chest. Her tongue danced lightly across his nipples, then down his stomach, as she knelt and took him into her mouth.

"Ohhh," Clint said, taking a deep breath and then lacing his fingers into her hair as he began to rotate his hips to the movement of her mouth as she sucked passionately.

When he could stand it no longer, when he was ready to explode, Clint stopped her. He scooped her up, laid her on the bed, then spread her legs apart, and his tongue darted out to find the soft, wet center of her pleasure. He heard her moan and then his tongue and his lips were doing things to her that soon had her pulling his head down into her and had her grinding her hips faster and faster until she cried out in ecstasy, "Oh, Clint! Clint!"

He let her buck until her stomach muscles stopped twitching and her legs lay still. Then, he pulled off his shirt, kicked out of his boots and pants, and stared down at her hungrily.

"Come and get it," she breathed, reaching for him.

Clint was only too happy to oblige her. It had been a long time and he was filled with a hunger for her that had been building from the moment he had first seen her across from his hotel window. He had wanted her then, and that had never changed.

She opened her legs wide for him. She was wet and she was hot. Clint knelt between her thighs and then they both watched as his manhood slowly penetrated her. When he felt the tip go inside, he started to pull back a little because he wanted to prolong this, make it good for both of them.

"No! Please," she begged, "do it now!"

And with that, she threw her legs up around his waist and pulled him into her with a savage urgency that could not be denied. Clint drove himself deep into her, feeling her hot slickness. Then, she began to hump and work him as her body moved with long, hard circles that seemed to come tighter and tighter.

He kissed her mouth and her neck and soon he forgot all about making anything last as their bodies fought and made love with growing intensity. He was driving himself into her and she was squealing with pleasure as he erupted, spurting his seed deep, his hips jackknifing out of control.

Later they lay still for a long time. Then, she was rolling herself on top of him, kissing his face and his chest. Rubbing his limpness into hardness and urging him to take her again. This time, she sat upright on him, head thrown back, breasts up and pointed, a thin mist of perspiration over her lovely body. A glazed look of passion shone in her eyes as she rode him up and down, then around and around, over and over until she was squealing like a cat and bouncing up and down wildly only to go rigid. Her lips pulled back in a smile and a moan came from deep within.

She fell forward and lay gasping. When she caught her breath, she looked down at him and said, ''I know what you think of me, and how you really don't even trust me. But I don't care. Before we get to Raton, you won't either. I'm going to love you so hard, you'll never want to let me go, Clint!''

He rolled her over on her back. His own hunger was not satisfied. ''We can start baiting Dudley tomorrow,'' he panted. ''That is, if either of us has the strength to walk after tonight.''

Then, he began to take her again. And this time, he would make it last a long, long time.

TWENTY-TWO

It was a cold, raw December day and Clint stood on the street corner feeling as old as he looked. Kathy had applied enough makeup to give the impression of deep facial lines, and his hair was talcum-powder white. His back ached from standing bent over all the time, and if one more sweet old lady tried to press a few coins into his hand as if he were some derelict or beggar, Clint was going to take his cane . . . well, he was going to bop her on the head.

For two days, Kathy had been on a shopping spree and he was beginning to wonder if they would have to form a wagon train to carry all the antiques, clothes, and trinkets down to Raton. He knew that she had one hell of a lot of money, but after watching her in action, he also knew that she was capable of spending it all before the week was out.

A single, beautiful woman always attracts attention and last night after dinner, a tall, dark man had foisted himself on her and had almost managed to force himself into their bedroom. And he would have, had not Clint finally gotten angry listening to his pleadings in the hallway and gone out to discourage him from taking any further liberties with Kathy.

There had been sharp words, and since he had been too weary to rid himself of his disguise, the stranger had ridiculed Clint as a dottering old fool and had threatened him with mayhem. The result was that Clint had thrown the handsome dandy down the staircase much to the shock of the hotel's genteel guests. The hotel management had been forced to call for a stretcher and a doctor. When they had demanded an explanation from Kathy, she said she could not imagine who the attacker was. She and her dear old father had heard a ruckus, but they had been wise enough to remain locked within their rooms.

Clint had smiled wearily and then made a feeble cackling sound deep in his throat. He had rolled his eyes and stuck out his tongue. The hotel manager had gaped with shock, then had retreated after apologizing profusely.

But today, Clint was growing impatient. He could not understand why Bill Dudley had not yet spotted Kathy— because it seemed like every other man in Denver had.

Right now, she was inside a huge emporium buying God only knew what else. She'd been in there for over two hours and Clint was chilled to the bone for the wind was freezing.

He studied the street and decided that he had waited long enough. It was already four o'clock, and because of the weather, there wasn't as much foot traffic as usual. Maybe tomorrow he would have to abandon his disguise and go hunting for Dudley and the hell with the idea of luring him with Kathy.

Clint tottered across the street, then entered the emporium. The clerk looked up with that copied grin clerks get after too many years waiting on others, and when Clint sneezed and blew his nose, the man's phony smile vanished.

"What do you want in here?" he demanded. "You don't look like you have enough money to eat with. Go on and get out of here!"

Clint ignored him. The interior of the building was filled with everything from jars of pickles to saddles and rocking chairs. He could not see Kathy. "Where is the young woman who came in here some time ago?" he demanded, dropping the timid and weak voice he'd been using.

"What business is it of yours?" The man grabbed his broom and rushed around the counter. "Now, get out of here you old bum or I'll sweep the floor with you!"

The oak cane Clint had been using was stout and he whipped it up right between the storekeeper's legs. The man's eyes bulged and his mouth flew open as he doubled up and dropped to his knees in agony.

Clint charged down the aisles and tore through row after row of merchandise, knocking displays and bolts of cloth spinning.

She was gone! He looked everywhere and then he saw the back door ajar. He raced over to discover that it had been padlocked closed, but the hasp had been pried away by a shiny new crowbar.

He charge out into an alley and wildly looked up and down. Nothing in sight!

"Hey!" he shouted, racing back up to the front of the store. "The woman is gone. Your back door was pried open. Was there a man in here?"

The clerk looked up. His face was still a little ashen, but now, instead of contempt, his face showed fright. "Who are you?" he choked. "You're not old."

Clint bent down and hauled him to his feet. "Was there a man in here with the woman!"

"Yes!" He cringed. "He was a big man, black hair, sharp features, had a scar along one cheek, but he was dressed good. Seemed pleasant. I got busy and forgot about them. What'd they steal?"

Clint dropped him and twisted for the front door. If Bill Dudley murders Kathy, it is all my fault, he thought miserably. Clint pitched his cane away and started running toward the hotel for no better reason than it was the only place where

Dudley might chose to go in order to get Kathy's money.

If they were there, then maybe there was still a chance to save Kathy's life and bring Dudley to justice, but if not . . . well, he did not even want to think about that possibility.

TWENTY-THREE

He did not care what the hotel clerk thought about a weird old man with white hair bounding up the staircase of the fancy hotel. Clint reached the top of the stairway and halted for just a moment to catch his breath. He unbuttoned his coat, and palmed his gun, and then tiptoed down the plushly carpeted hallway until he reached the room he and Kathy shared.

Pressing his ear to the door, he listened but heard nothing. Either Dudley was waiting with his gun trained on the entrance, or they were not there. Clint had no time to guess. He fitted his key into the lock, slowly turned it, then grasped the knob with his left hand while standing as far out of the line of fire as possible.

When he felt the knob lock, he took a deep breath, then threw the door open and jumped out of the line of fire. The shots he'd expected did not come. Clint peeked around the door with his gun ready. The room was demolished—and very empty.

"Damn!" he whispered, stepping inside to study the place.

All the drawers had been emptied and thrown on the floor. The mattress had been slit and stuffing was all over the room. Clint's own things were scattered and his bedroll, no longer neatly rolled, was turned inside out.

Bill Dudley had brought her back and ransacked the place. That much was clear. What wasn't entirely clear was where they'd gone next, but Clint had a notion they might try the bank where her savings were deposited.

He spun around and took for the stairs only to collide in the hallway with the desk clerk, whom he laid flat.

"Sorry!" Clint yelled as he charged down the stairs, through the lobby, and out the door.

Fortunately, the bank was only a few doors down the street and Clint reached it just as the manager was locking up.

"Quick! It's a matter of life or death. Did Miss Kathy Ault and a man come here to close her savings account?"

The bank manager was so startled by the sudden question and by Clint's wild appearance that he merely nodded.

"Did they say where they were going?"

"Of course not. It is none of our business . . . and, and," he spluttered, "what business is it of yours? Who are you?"

"Is there a train or a stagecoach leaving Denver soon?"

"Only the Denver Pacific and it's heading north to Cheyenne. It ought to be leaving"—he pulled out a heavy gold watch on an equally impressive gold chain—"about now, I'd say. Be nice if you were on it, whoever you are."

Clint ignored the insult. There was a horse tied at a nearby hitching rail and there was no time to run afoot all the way to the train station. Besides, he was bushed and he'd run about far enough to last for the next six months. So he untied the horse, swung into the saddle, and whipped the beast into a lumbering run. Now that his mind was on it, he thought he could hear the whistle blowing and he'd be damned if it didn't seem to be fading into the distance.

What he wouldn't give to have Duke instead of this plowhorse! Clint wasn't wearing spurs and he didn't have a quirt, so he tore his hat off and began to fan the horse's backside, making big popping noises. It shook the horse a little and made it gallop with all its might.

Clint almost trampled two women crossing the street and

a teamster gave him hell when he was forced to pull up short at a blind intersection. But Clint didn't care. He wasn't heading for the train station anymore; instead he was shooting at an angle that would intersect with the tracks just north of town and save him a good mile.

If he gambled right and caught the train, he was sure he would find Bill Dudley and Kathy. And if he didn't, all he'd lose was some time and whatever it took to keep himself from being charged with horse stealing if the owner of this nag returned before he did.

"Ya! Run, damn you! Move it!" he yelled, dusting the horse's backside harder and harder with his hat. "Yaaa!"

TWENTY-FOUR

The train was coming, and if this nag he was riding didn't quit on him, Clint figured he was going to intersect with the caboose in about two minutes.

Black smoke was pouring from the engine and he knew that the engineer was having coal thrown to the fire to build steam for the long, gradual climb toward the north. If the train had been on a downslope, the Gunsmith never would have caught it. But now, as he swept in, Clint guessed the train's speed was decreasing slightly just as his own was remaining somewhat steady.

He leaned out of the saddle and the horse shied away from the train just as he prepared to launch himself. If he had jumped, he'd have eaten railroad cinder. ''Ya!'' he yelled, drawing his gun and taking careful aim at the nag's haunches. There was nothing to lose; the train was inching away, and if the horse couldn't be made to give one final burst of speed, all was lost.

Clint said a silent prayer and pulled the trigger. His gun belched and the bullet seared through horsehide. The nag took wings and bolted for about twenty strides.

That was all Clint needed or wanted. He reached out, caught a handrail, and then threw himself out of the saddle to fall in a heap on the landing platform. Jumping to his feet, he burst into the caboose to find an old railroad man cowering behind a tin stove.

"Is this a holdup?"

"Hell, no," Clint growled as he pushed past him, moved the length of the caboose, threw the forward door open, and passed into the next coach.

Leaving the old man gaping, he moved from coach to coach.

He knew he looked wild and crazy. The makeup Kathy had used to give his face lines had begun to run with his sweat. The talcum powder in his hair had been rubbed off by the crown of his hat, so only the sides of his head were white. There was one other thing that made people stare and then shrink down in their seats: the gun in his fist.

There were six cars on the train and he caused a commotion in all of them as porters and conductors tried to stop him, then fell back in his wake as he moved on, examining every face.

He had Bill Dudley's description—tall, black hair, scar down one cheek, and if the man were on the train, he figured he was going to take him alive if possible, but dead if necessary. Dudley had caused Clint too much grief.

When he burst into the dining car, he saw them at the same instant that Kathy saw him. The shock was so great that she dropped the glass of wine she'd been holding to her lips and it crashed on to her plate as she cried, "Clint!"

It was the wrong thing to do, but there was no helping it. Clint raised his gun, but there were three tables of diners between him and Dudley and no clear line of fire.

At the same instant, Dudley whirled around in his chair and his hand dropped for his own gun. Clint yelled, "Everybody down!"

Three tables of people dived for the floor.

Both guns exploded at the same instant and Dudley spun around to collide with a porter carrying a tray of food. The tray crashed, and just as Clint was about to yell for Dudley to freeze, the man grabbed the porter and spun him around for a shield.

"Drop it or this man dies, Gunsmith!"

Clint eased up on his trigger. The porter was an old black gentleman and all had to admire his composure. He stood frozen with Dudley's forearm locked around his neck and gun to his temple.

"If this man's a killer, then you go ahead and shoot," the porter said bravely.

Clint lowered his gun slowly. "I can't," he said.

"Drop it!"

Clint let the gun slip from his fingers.

Bill Dudley grinned. He was big and athletic, handsome enough to have been a leading man on some stage. He had a square jaw and his eyes glinted as hard and as bright as obsidian. Looking at him as he smiled, Clint thought once more about how Kathy had once been his lover and it made sense. She, too, was beautiful and they'd have made a striking pair. The contrast between Dudley and her own miserly, far older husband must have been inescapable. Clint could not help wondering again if they had been in cahoots from the very beginning. Certainly, when he had barged into this dining car, Kathy had been enjoying herself in the man's company.

Dudley shook his head. "Gave you a second chance to live. Not many get that from me. You should have taken it and stayed in Denver. Gone on your way in peace. Too bad."

"Bill, please," Kathy pleaded, "don't kill him."

"Got to. This is the famous Gunsmith. You think he'll just let me tie him up and then get off in Cheyenne and ride away free? Hell, no! He'd hunt me to the grave. Isn't that right?"

Clint nodded grimly.

"See. Got to kill him. Then, it's just you and me."

Clint's eyes locked with Kathy's. He looked deep into them, trying to read, trying to imagine her thoughts, where her heart and her loyalties lay. Clint had often been told he was very appealing to the opposite sex, but he knew he wasn't as handsome as the man who was about to kill him.

"Well, Kathy," he said, "now that we've come to this, which is it?"

Dudley knocked the porter to the floor as he reached out and pulled her close. "She's mine!"

"I asked her," Clint said softly.

Before she could answer, Dudley slapped her across the face, knocking her into their table and spilling everything to the floor.

"Move!" he ordered, pointing his gun at Clint's chest. "We are going to take a little walk outside."

"Bill, no!"

"Shut up! I told you I have no choice!"

Kathy shrank back and then Clint was being shoved through the door to stand between the coaches.

"So long, Gunsmith. Killing you will be a real feather in my cap."

Clint glanced down at the blurring landscape. The train was moving full speed now, but he knew that he was either going to lunge at Dudley or throw himself off into space and hope that the impact of his body against the ground wouldn't prove fatal.

I'll go for him, Clint thought. To hell with it. "Just one thing . . ."

He had meant to gain some momentary diversion, but it wasn't necessary. Because suddenly, Bill Dudley was arching his back as gunfire exploded in the dining car. Dudley tried to turn, tried to lift his own gun.

"You . . . Judas!" he choked.

Then, the gun in Kathy's hand exploded once more and

Bill Dudley's body went sailing off the platform to crash, roll, and lie very still. Looking back down the track, Clint thought Dudley looked like a broken doll, one thrown out the window by some pampered rich girl.

When Clint turned back, Kathy's head was in her hands and she was sobbing. Maybe someday, sometime, he'd find out if she and Dudley had conspired to kill Mr. Todd, but right now it just didn't seem to matter.

When the chips were down, Kathy had made the right choice.

TWENTY-FIVE

The trip south to Raton was almost two hundred miles. Clint drove a four-horse team with Kathy perched on the seat beside him and Duke tied up behind. It would take them a full week, but since it was only mid-December, he did not mind the time, even though he could have made it on horseback in four days.

They stayed at inns and small boarding houses along the way and they ate and rested well. At night, they made love passionately and during the days, they talked of many things. It became clear to Clint that Kathy wanted to remarry, and that she hoped he would be her man. In as gentle a way as possible, he told her that he had no intention of settling down and that he did not have the money it would take to satisfy a woman with her taste for expensive things.

"I don't care about that, Clint. I can live simply."

He laughed and jerked his thumb back to the huge load of furniture, clothes, and household goods she had bought in just the few days she'd been in Denver. "Kathy, living simply is a log cabin and handmade furniture. It's making do with what you need and not worrying about what color your tablecloth is or how the couch matches the rug. You don't want that kind of simple."

"Well," she hedged, "you may be right. I can't see myself scrubbing clothes on a washboard beside a river or making tallow candles and things like that. But you don't seem that simple kind of man. You are too sophisticated, too worldly a traveler to be content stuck out on some barren section of land.''

''True,'' he conceded, ''but I don't care about fancy things or money the way you do. Mark my words, Kathy, you are already a wealthy woman, and if you ever learn how to save a little money, you always will be.''

''I've had enough saving! Mr. Todd spent his whole life saving and cheating people out of their money and look what it got him. Nope, Clint, I want to have a little fun. But first, I'm going to open an antique store in Raton and get a business going. Then, when the money rolls in, I plan to travel. Want to come?''

He smiled. ''We'll see. Right now my main concern is what I can do to help old Pete.''

''I hope you don't have to shoot anyone else.''

''So do I,'' he said, ''but when people call on the Gunsmith, it has an unfortunate way of getting around to that kind of business.''

''Well, let's hope that this time is different.''

Clint nodded. He could hope, but he doubted it would be. Generally speaking, a man did not ask his best friend to come nearly a thousand miles across mountains in the middle of winter just to help him build a new barn.

Raton was a bustling mining and ranching town high up in the mountains. It showed great promise and had grown a good deal since Clint's last visit. Now, there were churches, a newspaper, three entire blocks of permanent houses, and a schoolhouse.

Downtown, there was a definite air of prosperity. Cafés and saloons, two saddle shops, and any number of general stores all competed for a rapidly expanding trade along this stop on the old Santa Fe Trail.

"I like it!" Kathy said as they rode down the impressive main street past the many businesses. "And I don't see a single antique store."

Clint didn't comment. To his mind, the antique trade might be a little slow in a town this size. Bu they had passed some pretty impressive Victorian homes and those kinds of places might have owners interested in antiques.

"Well," he said, pulling the brake, "this is it."

"This?"

He jumped to the street and then helped her down. "Yep. Finest saloon in Raton, I'd say. And look at the sign. Says that Pete still owns it."

He pointed to his friend's name on the Hot Lizard Saloon sign. It caused Clint to relax a little, figuring that if Pete had gotten into financial trouble and had to sell everything, his name would not be on the sign anymore.

"Come on inside, Kathy. You'll like Pete."

She shook her head. "No," she decided, "if I'm to become a businesswoman in this town, it would be better if I am not seen by the town ladies entering a saloon the moment I arrive."

"Suit yourself," he said, "but it will be warmer inside than it is out here in the wind."

"I have extra clothes to wear if I need them."

Clint thought about all the trunks and boxes packed with new clothes. Kathy had that much right. This woman had enough clothing to outfit the biggest bordello in New Orleans.

Nothing had changed inside the Hot Lizard. Same twenty-foot polished mahogany bar with its brass footrail, same pictures of plump, cherubic, nude women and old sailing ships tossing about in terrible ocean storms. The piano looked a little more scarred, but the kerosene lamps that hung from the ceilings were as garish as ever.

"Well, I'll be damned!" Fred the bartender beamed. "As I live and breathe, it's the Gunsmith!"

A half dozen patrons looked up and grinned. Several of those he recognized came over to shake his hand. Drinks were set up on the bar and the whiskey was even better than he remembered.

"Well, where is the old bastard?" Clint grinned.

The smiles died.

"What's wrong?" Clint set his drink down untouched.

"Take it easy." The bartender swallowed. "Pete is dying of a gunshot wound. He was ambushed about three months ago and, for a while, we thought he was going to pull out of it just fine. But he isn't. Doctor said the bullet paralyzed him from the waist down and he'll never walk again. Old Pete, you know the kind of man he is. He'd rather be dead than have to be half a man."

"Where is he now?" Clint whispered, feeling his throat squeezing tight.

"Upstairs. Same room he's always had. Pete owns two or three of the best houses in town. He could afford about anything he wants, only he likes to stay close to the bar's action. Likes to hear the piano playing at night and the laughter of our customers. He always did."

Clint nodded. He took the bottle of whiskey and two glasses and headed for the stairs. Pete's was by far the largest room, second door on the right.

He had always kept a few women working up there, and he was good to them, too. Everyone knew that if any hurt one of Pete's girls, he'd better ride a fast horse out of Raton and hope to hell Pete never caught him.

When he came to the door, he knocked softly.

"Who the hell is it?"

Clint opened the door and stepped inside, closing it behind him. The man in the bed wasn't the man he'd remembered, the one who'd saved his life and been accused of raising more hell in New Mexico than anyone. No. The man he saw now looked small and shrunken, wasted by sickness and inactivity but mostly by pain.

He blinked in the dimness and Clint stepped forward until he was standing right up next to the bed. "Well, you old son of a bitch, you gonna have a drink with me?"

"Gunsmith, it's you!" Pete choked, reaching up with both hands. His arms were all big bone and tendon covered by wasted flesh.

Clint took his hand and forced a smile. "Whatever you meant by *urgent* had damn sure better be *urgent*," he said. "Just wait until I tell you the hell I've gone through getting here."

"Glad you came."

"So am I, old friend. If I'd a known you were in this kind of fix, I'd have gotten here even sooner. Fred told me about the gunshot. I want to know who did it."

"Pour us a drink. There is plenty of time to get to that business. Let's talk of the old days, the good times when we fought well. Remember them damn Tater brothers? I never forgot them."

Pete downed his whiskey and licked his lips. "Keep pouring, Clint. A full bottle always did make me thirsty."

Clint poured again. So far, Pete Haywood had avoided talking about what had happened. But give him a little time and half a bottle of whiskey, and Clint knew that he would open up and tell his story—who had shot him and was responsible for his dying slowly like this.

Clint would drink with him, glass for glass. There was time. Retribution would come soon enough.

TWENTY-SIX

"It's this way," Pete said, eyes shining feverishly. "After that day you rode through the pass and little Zeb and me killed the Tater brothers, we got a warning that, sooner or later, me and Zeb would be killed. Turns out that the Taters had some kinfolk in Arizona. They was all locked up in the Yuma pen. So six months ago two of them got out. They are part of the Wadsworth clan."

"Wadsworth clan?" The name sounded familiar. There had been some Wadsworths down in Arizona, and from what Clint remembered, they'd been a vicious gang.

"Yeah," Pete said, "they are distant cousins to the Taters. But when we shot the Taters, the Wadsworths just took it up as a blood feud."

"So they are the ones who ambushed you."

"I'm sure of it, though there were no witnesses. You see, one of them challenged Zeb to a gunfight. Challenged him right out in front of everyone. I knew he is damn fast with a gun—and Zeb isn't—so I tried to go in Zeb's place. But he wouldn't hear of it."

"Pride," Clint said. "I'm not surprised. Be tough to live in a town where your father went and did your fighting."

"Yeah," Pete said tiredly. "I knew that, too. But what is a man supposed to do? Let his son go out and get shot down in the street by a gunfighter who'd give him no chance at all?"

"I wouldn't let my son face a man who was clearly faster.

It's murder. So what did you do, Pete? Kill this Wadsworth fella all on your own?''

"Sorta, only I did it so that it would look to everyone here in Raton that Zeb outdrew the man fair and square.''

"Mind telling me how you accomplished that?''

"Easy. I was hiding in an empty barrel when they faced each other in the street. I just poked my gun through a knothole and fired a second before that Wadsworth did. It worked out just dandy.''

Clint smiled. "That's damn clever.''

"I think so, too!'' Pete's eyes glistened. "And you should have seen my boy. He'd been expecting to die out there, and when the other man went down, he just couldn't hardly believe his eyes. He was the happiest young fella in all of New Mexico. I had to stay in the barrel until it got dark so I could sneak out, but it was worth it.''

"So what went wrong?''

Pete's smile faded and his expression became bleak. "Zeb got big-headed. One day he was just a big, nice, easygoing fella who happened to be the son of the wealthiest man in town; the next he was a gunfighter. He lost his head. All the prettiest young women suddenly started seeing him as if he was something special and his friends began to treat him with . . . well, you know how most people treat you.''

Clint nodded. When you were a famous gunfighter, you found that people either wanted to be your friend, or they went out of their way to keep their distance. They just did not act normal. A top gunman had to have his head screwed on right or he could easily get swell-headed by the attention he received.

"So Zeb forgot who he really was. He started swaggering around a little, bragging a little. Hell, I was ashamed of him for the first time in my life—until I got to thinking how everyone had always feared and respected me for my fighting abilities and my son never got any respect at all. Suddenly, he was his own man.''

"You tried to talk to him.''

Pete poured another round for them. "Sure,'' he said. "But I couldn't rightly tell him that I'd climbed into a barrel and shot his man from hiding, could I?''

"No,'' Clint said slowly, "that would have made him hate you, would have shamed him and broken his spirit.''

Pete nodded. "I knew you'd understand, Clint. You are young enough still to remember what fools we were until we got seasoned. And we were lucky enough to live that long. Problem is, I'm afraid Zeb won't have that same chance. He's all I got left, Clint. He gets killed, my whole life will seem like a waste.''

"Why should he get killed?'' Clint asked softly, moved by the desperation in Pete's voice.

"Because I made him think he is a gunfighter, a man fast on the draw. And he isn't! I always avoided gunfighting around him because we've both seen what usually happens to fellas his age when they start practicing with a gun all the time. Sooner or later—usually sooner—they get to bragging and take on a real shooter who sends them straight up to Boot Hill.''

"You want me to talk to him?''

"I'm afraid that won't be enough anymore.'' Pete took a ragged breath. "The man who ambushed me is a Wadsworth and he is just waiting for more of them to get sprung from Yuma. Then, they plan to face Zeb in the street and kill him.''

"I'll take his place,'' Clint said. "Don't worry.''

"You can't! Don't you see that it would destroy him! All he does is practice with a gun. He'd never run away.''

"Then, he and I will stand against them together.''

"He's no good,'' Pete whispered. "You'd be facing them

alone. You see, Zeb had his hand crushed in a mining accident about five years ago. I should never have let him go to work, but he wanted to earn his own money, get away from me for a summer. So I let him and he came home with a hand all smashed up. It healed, but the doctor said there are some tendons inside that won't mend right and so he can't use the hand like he normally would.''

Clint swallowed. ''Can't he see that?''

''He used to be able to. But since he outdrew and killed that Wadsworth fella, he can't see nothing straight anymore. I'm ashamed of him acting like he does, but I know he'll come out of it one of these days because he's a fine young man—or was until this happened.''

''So what can I do to help?'' The situation seemed almost hopeless. He couldn't tell Zeb the truth, and he couldn't even expect to teach him how to become fast enough to face up to a man in an open gunfight.

''I don't know,'' Pete said, tears making his eyes glisten. ''But . . . but I've heard that two more Wadsworth men get out of prison at Christmas and it'll take them a week or two to get to Raton. I just thought we might be able to put our heads together and think of something.''

''We will,'' Clint heard himself say. ''Don't worry, we won't let your boy get killed out in the street.''

Pete grabbed him by the shoulder and his grip was as weak as that of a child. ''I knew you'd help! Knew you'd think of some way out of this! By God, Clint, that boy is all I have in the world. I own a fair part of downtown, and he'll be wealthy after I die. I want him to have his inheritance and live to enjoy it!''

''I'll do my best. How old is he now?''

''Twenty-one next month. I want to hang on until that one, then . . .''

The knock at the door made them both turn around.

"Who is it?" Pete yelled.

"Kathy. Miss Kathy Ault. Is Clint in there?"

Pete smiled. "You harnessed to a woman?"

"Had no choice but to bring her along."

"Let me take a look at her. I always did admire your taste in females. Be good to see if you have kept it up."

Clint stood. "All right. But watch out, Pete. This woman has a mind of her own. Intends to open an antique store here in Raton and become a businesswoman."

"Well, my, my! Let's have a look."

Clint let her in, feeling certain that his old friend was going to be impressed. Kathy was a hell of a looker and underneath all those winter clothes, there was a figure that would make any man lick his lips.

TWENTY-SEVEN

Clint could tell from the sudden sparkle in Pete's eyes that his old friend was impressed by Kathy. Though it did not show now, Pete had once been quite a ladies' man himself in his younger days and his appreciation for a lovely woman had obviously not diminished with his failing health.

"Come over here and sit down beside me," Pete said to her, waving her closer.

"It got too cold out there on the seat of that wagon, Clint. I had to come inside and get warm."

Her eyes filled with deep concern when she studied the man lying in bed. "And you must be Pete Haywood. It's a great honor to meet such a famous man as yourself, Mr. Haywood."

She offered her hand, and looking at Pete, Clint knew she had already completely charmed the old devil.

"Aw," he said almost shyly, "I never was that famous. The Gunsmith is the one everybody knows. Me, well, I just have a local reputation is all."

"Don't be overly modest," Kathy said, taking a chair at his bedside. "Clint has told me how you saved his life that day in the pass and how fearless you have always been in the face of danger. I am sorry to see that you are not feeling well and hope that you might get better soon."

"Seeing a woman as pretty as you sure won't hurt any." Pete beamed. He looked at Clint. "You always did have the best women I ever saw—and the sweetest, too. Sure wish my son, Zeb, would stumble on to one like this. He has something to learn about class, that boy. Seeing this here lady ought to be a real education for Zeb, who thinks with that thing hanging between his legs.''

Pete smiled self-consciously. "I'm sorry, Miss . . .''

"Ault. Kathy Ault.''

"You must forgive me my crude manners. Around here, I live among drunks, whores, and fools for the main part.''

"You have nothing to be apologizing for, Mr. Haywood. I am a woman who has, I'm afraid, seen the dark side of life. I am no gilded lily, not at all.''

Pete patted her hand. "No, I didn't expect you were, traveling with Clint. No offense meant, Clint.''

"None taken,'' he answered with an grin of amusement. He sat back and listened to them chatter away for a while, amazed that they found so much to discuss. Mostly Pete wanted to know more about Kathy's plans for opening an antique shop.

"I own most of this city block; I can rent you a prime store, and because you are Clint's woman and such a pretty thing, I'll let you have it practically for nothing the first year just so you can get off to a good start.''

"Well, thank you! I would sincerely appreciate that.'' Kathy's eyes were shining as brightly as if he had just given her the city itself. "I just know that I'm going to love it here in Raton. It is beautiful and all the men in your saloon seemed so friendly.''

"I'll bet,'' Clint said dryly. "While you and Pete are talking all about the art of making a business pay, I think I'll go find Zeb and catch up on old times.''

"Yes!'' Pete said. "Why don't you do that! You're that young man's hero and you always have been.''

Clint smiled modestly. "Hate to spoil an illusion, but I'd

better go visit him anyway. Any idea where I might find him?''

Pete scowled. ''Much as I hate to say it, he'll probably be at Rosie's Place. That's where he spends whatever time he has when he's not practicing to become a famous gunman. I have no idea who his latest love is, but I do know that she is paid well. That boy costs me a damn hefty share of the profits from the Hot Lizard each week.''

Clint stopped at the door. The Pete Haywood he knew would never have allowed his son to take advantage of him this way. But then, when a man is dying and all he has is one son, who can blame him from going weak out of a desire to keep the peace. Still and all, the idea of young Zeb spending time and money in a cathouse and away from his father did not sit well with the Gunsmith; he'd expected more from Zeb.

Maybe Pete read his troubled thoughts because he said, ''Don't judge Zeb too hard, Clint. The boy never had a mother, just a parade of women I kept turning over, one after the other. None of them cared a damn about him and I don't think he knows what a real woman is capable of doing for a man she really loves. And with this gunfight thing hanging over Zeb, well . . . well, I guess maybe deep inside he's scared, though he'd never admit it to anyone. He thinks he has to live up to my reputation with a gun, and he never will.''

''Those days are nearly over; we both know that.''

Pete nodded. ''You tell that to the Wadsworth boys when they come gunning.''

''I'll be here,'' Clint said as he passed out into the hallway, ''and I'll get the message across one way or the other.''

Outside, the air was filled with blowing snow and it was plain that they were in for a storm. Clint climbed on to the wagon and drove it to the livery where he paid the man to unhitch the team and keep the wagon tarped and safe. There was a lot of Kathy's money tied up in that wagon and he wanted to take no chance of losing it.

"You go about your business," he said, leading Duke to a stall filled with fresh straw, "I'll take care of my horse right now."

He put the horse inside and then inspected Duke's legs. They looked fine. The wounds were nearly all gone and he rubbed some bacon fat over the new flesh to promote hair growth. In another month, he was confident that Duke would not have a mark on him.

Clint received directions to Rosie's Place and lowered his head to barge into the driving wind. It had been almost seven years since he had last seen the boy, and he knew that he wouldn't even recognize him on the street. Zeb wasn't a boy anymore, and from all accounts, he was pretty mixed up and headed for a lot of trouble. The best thing Zeb could do, Clint thought, was to ride away and stay away for a while until things blew over. But then, if I were Zeb, I wouldn't run either, Clint thought. I guess we will just have to stay and face the music.

TWENTY-EIGHT

Rosie's Place was about three cuts above most whorehouses and clearly it appealed to the better class of men in Raton. The sitting room was tastefully decorated in soft greens and blues and the saloon had an air of elegance. At least six pretty young women were sitting there socializing with customers, some of whom wore business suits and looked like lawyers or bankers.

There was no hustle. When Clint had come inside, Rosie herself had greeted him warmly and offered to buy him a drink on the house. She took his coat and hat and put them in a cloak room with the assurance that they would be safe. She suggested that Clint check his gun there, too, but he declined, and when he walked inside, several men recognized him at once. That upset Rosie until Clint promised her that he was not expecting trouble but that a man with his past had too many enemies to take the chance of going into public unarmed.

Zeb was not inside the saloon, but Clint took a seat anyway and sat down with the madam, a woman in her early forties who looked trim and in surprisingly good shape considering her background.

When the bartender had poured his and Rosie's drink, Clint said, "Mighty nice place you have here."

"Thank you!" She winked. "But the best part is upstairs. Do you see a girl you'd like to join us?"

"Actually I'm looking for a young man by the name of Zeb Haywood. His father said he'd likely be here."

"Upstairs with Susie as usual." Rosie sighed. "Susie used to be my best girl, until Zeb took a shine to her. Now . . . well, you know how it is."

"Can't say as I do."

"Zeb is the son of Pete Haywood who is just about the most powerful man here in Raton. I wouldn't dream of kicking his boy out in the street. Besides, when old Pete cashes in, Zeb is going to be worth a lot of money."

"From what I hear, Zeb already spends plenty here."

Rosie's dark eyes flashed with sudden anger. "He spends mostly just his time here! This isn't no boardinghouse. I'm in business to made a profit, not take in the homeless."

Clint sipped his drink. It was watered down pretty good, but he didn't care. He'd come for business, not pleasure. "If you feel that way, you really should go and tell Pete. He appreciates honesty."

"You can't tell me anything about that man that I don't already know, Gunsmith. Pete and I have smoked a few bedsheets together."

"I see."

"And it isn't that I don't like Zeb, because I do. I guess when he outdrew that man in the street, I was just as surprised and happy as anyone. Zeb is a damned likeable young man. He hasn't a mean bone in his body and he is always laughing about something. Has a real nice sense of humor, or at least he did until he got so swell-headed. I just wish he was the way he used to be before all this happened. The Wadsworth boys are going to kill him for sure."

"I might have something to say about that," Clint drawled.

"So that's why you have come here? To face the Wadsworth men?"

"If I have to."

"You will. They'll back down from no one, not even you, Gunsmith. And they'll shoot you from behind like they did to Pete, if they can."

"I'll watch my back pretty close." Clint finished his drink. "Well, guess I better go up there and pay him a visit."

"They're in room three; better knock first."

"Of course. Nice talking to you, Rosie. Thanks for the drink."

"Next time, I hope we can show you some real fun upstairs," she said.

"I never pay for it. Just a matter of foolish pride I guess, and I don't intend to start now."

She laid her hand over his. "Whiskey isn't the only thing that is on the house to my special friends. You come back soon, hear now?"

"I may just do that after all," he told her.

He knocked on the door and the creaking of the springs didn't stop, so he waited a few minutes and when he grew impatient, he pushed inside.

Zeb was riding Susie for all he was worth, and from the tempo of the action, Clint guessed nothing was going to stop them until they were finished. They hadn't even noticed him, so he walked quietly over to the window and studied the street below. It was snowing harder and he was glad that he and Kathy were here and not caught out on the trail in this mess.

"Oh, oh, Zeb!" Susie squealed with ecstasy.

"Yeah! Yeah!" he cried as their bodies locked and strained.

Clint kept his eyes on the street until the bedsprings fell silent. When he turned around, the young pair were lying spent in each other's arms. "Uh-hem," he said, clearing his throat noisily.

Zeb came off his woman and scrambled for his gun, which was draped over the bedpost, and Clint just barely grabbed it first.

"Easy now," he said, studying the tall, slender young man who stood crouched and as naked as the day he was born. "Don't you remember me?"

"Hell no! What are you doing in here!"

"I came a long way to see you and your father. I'm the Gunsmith."

The fierce anger and outrage on Zeb's handsome young face melted and he stood up slowly. "You're the Gunsmith?"

Clint handed him his gun, noting how someone had filed the front sight down so that it would come out of a holster quicker. "That's right."

"Susie, this is the man I've told you about so often. It's really him!"

Susie was a brunette, plump and pretty with dark eyes and a sultry sexiness that would attract most any young man. In ten years she would be fat and sloppy and mean, but Zeb couldn't see that now and Clint could not blame him. Susie was ripe and obviously ready. Her smile was inviting, her eyes covered him from head to toe, and the invitation indicated she was ready whenever he was.

"It's an honor," she said, reaching out for his hand and letting the sheets fall into her lap so that he could see her breasts, which were worth an eyeful.

He declined her hand but said, "Thank you, Susie." Then, turning to Zeb, "Why don't you get dressed and you and I can go over to your father's saloon and get reacquainted?"

Zeb was already grabbing for his underclothes. "Well, sure! Honey, you don't mind, do you?"

She did mind. Clint saw the pout form on her lips. "Rosie

don't want me up here alone, you know that.''

"Well, damn it, I'll be back in an hour or two. Put it on ice, huh?''

"You don't need to be crude, Zeb. He doesn't, does he, Mr. Gunsmith?'' She smiled again and licked her lips with mock sensuality.

Clint almost laughed outright. Susie had the mind and the thoughts of a spoiled little child. She had probably not been in this business long and still held some of the illusions of a girl. Give her a little time and all this silly coyness would wash away like dirt off socks.

"What you do with your time is up to you, Susie.''

"You're no help.''

Not yet I'm not, Clint thought. But if getting him to see that he's wasting his time on you counts for anything, then I sure will be.

They had taken a table against the back wall of the Hot Lizard and opened a bottle of the best the saloon had to offer. Clint had been talking for more than an hour, but he might just as well have been spitting into the wind.

"Look,'' he said tiredly, "I didn't come to fight your battles or steal your thunder; it's just that you are all that your father has and he doesn't want you to die.''

"I'm not going to die. I'm fast and I got what it takes to make me a reputation with a gun.''

"Forget the damned reputation! I've got one and I try to live it down every day of my life. Do you think I enjoy being looked upon as some kind of god, or else having to try to talk every drunken fool who thinks he's good out of drawing a gun and proving it? I spend more time avoiding trouble than I do in peace. You don't want a reputation. Men who are fast, really fast, haven't a need for one—it's only the guys who feel something lacking inside themselves who go around bragging how fast they are, who want and need that attention.''

Zeb struggled to his feet. He had been drinking too fast and now it showed. ''Are you saying that I am that kind of man?''

Clint groaned. ''Sit down,'' he said, grabbing Zeb by the arm and pulling him back into his seat.

''I didn't say or mean that at all. You've got nothing to prove, nothing to gain, and everything to lose.''

''I ain't running from the Wadsworths! Is that what my father wanted you to ask me to do?''

''No. He understands you could never put your tail between your legs and run. He just wishes you would—''

''Would what?'' Zeb asked with exasperation. ''Either I run or I fight. There's no other choice that I can see. Can you?''

''One.''

''What is it?''

''Let me help you.''

''You mean fight my battles?''

''No, I mean teach you a few tricks. Your father said you had a serious hand injury and that you—''

''My hand is fine! Didn't I prove that when I killed Elmer Wadsworth!''

''Simmer down,'' Clint said easily. ''I just meant there are ways to compensate for almost anything. It isn't always the fastest man who wins. Just as often, it's the one who fights smart, who doesn't panic and makes sure that all the odds are in his favor when he steps out into the street or walks into a saloon.''

Zeb relaxed, but his face was still wary. ''Listen, you are a legend and I'm not foolish enough to pass up your help. But I want you to know this; when they come, I'll be the one who goes out to face them, and I'll do it alone. Do you understand?''

Clint knew he had no choice for the moment but to agree. Any other answer would send young Zeb stomping back to Susie and this chance would be gone forever.

"All right," he said with deep reluctance. "I'll offer my professional knowledge, not my gun, to you for now."

"Then, we got a deal," Zeb said, visibly relaxing in his chair. "In two days, it'll be Christmas. I guess we had better get started pretty soon."

"Tomorrow morning," Clint said, rising to his feet. "Now, why don't you come upstairs and visit with my lady friend and your father for a while."

Zeb actually turned his head in the direction of Rosie's, but he resisted and joined Clint. They headed for the stairs.

Clint was frowning. Zeb was as proud and as stubborn as his father. This wasn't going to be easy, especially if his hand were physically damaged.

He was not looking forward to tomorrow—or to Christmas in Raton.

TWENTY-NINE

Clint placed a line of beer bottles on the snow-covered ridge and trudged back to Zeb. The snow had stopped blowing, but it was bitterly cold and a sane man would be hugging a potbellied stove or rock fireplace. But he had to find out just how good Zeb was and their time for practice was going to run out in just a few short weeks when the Wadsworth men arrived. No one even knew for sure how many of them were coming—two from prison for sure, but they might bring more with them to New Mexico to settle their debt.

Zeb was not pleased about being out either. He looked miserable and bored. "I can't show you anything now," he complained. "I got two sweaters on under this coat and I can barely bend my arm, much less draw a gun."

"Then, you had better take them off," Clint said, his breath forming clouds of vapor. "I need to see what you've got."

Zeb groaned. He took off his heavy buffalo robe and then one of the two sweaters. He was still wearing a wool shirt and longjohns underneath. "If I take off my gloves, my hands will stiffen in this weather. It's not a true test when your fingers are half frozen."

"A gunman has to be ready for action at all times. Conditions are rarely perfect when the moment comes to draw your gun and kill or be killed. You have to learn to overcome those kinds of things."

163

Zeb bit off his glove and flexed his hands. "You're talking about being steady, being mentally tough. Well, I am, but thinking your hands are warm and your fingers able to bend don't make it so, Gunsmith."

"Try them right now. Turn and face those beer bottles and let's see exactly what you can do."

Zeb started forward.

"Whoa!" Clint yelled. "Where are you going?"

"Damn things are too far away. Hell, Gunsmith, I been practicing my draw on a cottonwood tree that's as big around as a man. Not little bitty things like bottles."

"Come on back. You have to be able to do more than just hit an opponent. You have to place a bullet where it will drop him in his tracks. A wounded man can kill you, and if he knows he's going to die, sometimes he's most dangerous. One shot, and when you have to, you make it count."

"That ain't what I heard. I heard that if—"

"Look," he snapped, "you are the student and I am the teacher. You listen and I talk. We don't debate the finer points of gunfighting because you don't know anything. Later on, you can take my advice or ignore it, but right now, you take it. Understood?"

Clint was growing angry. He had not come out in this weather to argue with a kid who knew nothing about gunfighting.

He had purposefully been rough and now he had also made Zeb angry and that was good. It would get him fired up enough to start thinking about the business at hand.

"Hell, yes!" Zeb barked. He stopped and his hand went down to cover his holster. Then, he made his draw.

His hand seemed to Clint to move as if pulled on wires and pulleys. His movement was jerky and nowhere near as fast as Clint had hoped. The gun came up and Zeb fanned the trigger with the palm of his left hand before the barrel was on target.

His bullet ripped into the snow a good ten feet before the line of bottles and then Zeb was fanning his hammer and spraying the entire line. Of four bottles, one shattered.

Zeb actually grinned and to Clint's horror he twirled his empty gun on his finger as he brought his gun down so that it spun right into his holster. It was just the kind of stupid, showoff thing some kid might do. Clint was made a little ill by the entire display.

"Well," Zeb said proudly, "I know I missed a couple, but I am fast, aren't I? And considering the temperature, I think I did myself pretty damn proud."

Clint had turned away to hide his expression until he got himself under control. My God, he thought, the kid is awful!

"Gunsmith?"

He turned around. The last thing he should do would be to humiliate this foolish young man and squash his enormous pride. Clint took a deep breath. "It . . . it was fine," he managed to say, "but I do think there is some room for improvement."

Zeb frowned. He struggled with himself and managed to say graciously, "Maybe so, Gunsmith. I mean, even you can improve. Why don't you let me see if you can hit those bottles?"

Clint started to draw and then checked his hand.

If he demonstrated to Zeb how a real gunman could draw and fire, that might completely destroy Zeb's confidence. So he made his play at half speed and purposefully missed the last bottle twice before he nailed it.

"Wow! That was really something, Gunsmith!"

"Thanks," Clint managed to say as he reloaded. "You know, I never held much faith in the way some men fan their hammers. I'd like to see you learn to work the trigger like the gun was intended to be worked."

"Hell," Zeb grinned, "trigger doesn't work. I had a

gunsmith freeze it so there'd be no accident.''

"Let me see.''

Zeb was telling the truth. The young fool really had had the trigger frozen solid. That made the gun worthless in Clint's opinion. "What if you ever needed to aim at someone at a distance? Your sights are gone, and you damn sure couldn't hit anything fanning.''

"That's what rifles are for, Gunsmith. For a distance shot, I'd get a rifle. You being a gunfighter, I know you can see the sense in it. When the action starts, accuracy don't mean much. Most fighters are within twenty feet of each other. Just point and shoot. Point and shoot. That's all you need to learn once you got the speed down.''

"Did your father tell you that?''

"Hell, no! He'd never tell me anything about gunfighting. If it was up to him, I'd never have learned a damn thing and I'd be buried up on Boot Hill right now with Elmer Wadsworth's bullet in my chest. Nope, I learned it all from Texas Jack, an old gunfighter who lives east of town. He sure knows what the hell he's talking about. Man has the scars of four bullet holes on his body. Showed me all but one, that being near his personals.''

"I see. I'd like to meet this Texas Jack one of these days. He's supposed to be pretty good, huh?''

"One of the best. He's past his prime now, but he can twirl a sixshooter on his finger so fast it's a spinning blur. Does all sorts of fancy tricks with a gun. Everybody buys him drinks just to watch the show. Tomorrow being Christmas, I'm sure Texas Jack will ride into town and celebrate at our saloon.''

"Well,'' Clint said tightly, "I can hardly wait to meet this famous gunfighter myself.''

"You and Texas Jack, you wouldn't . . .''

"Wouldn't what, Zeb?''

"Well, you know, try to prove once and for all which of

you is the fastest. From what I just saw, you might beat him, but it wouldn't be fair, him being old now.''

Clint nodded. ''I see what you mean. No, I don't think there is much chance old Texas Jack and I would settle the question. You don't have to prove you're fast everytime you meet an equal.''

''Wow!'' Zeb exclaimed. ''Texas Jack said almost the same thing one time when someone tried to brace him and he just walked away. Takes nerves of steel to turn your back on someone who wants to kill you and then to forgive the man enough to allow him to go on living.''

Clint wanted to gag. ''Sure does. Look, why don't you and I practice again the day after Christmas? It's a little cold today.''

''Sure,'' Zeb said happily as he began putting on his sweater and coat. ''I guess I surprised you with how fast I am. Ain't that right, Gunsmith?''

''You sure did, son. You damn sure did.''

Zeb Haywood almost danced he was so pleased. It wasn't everyday a person won the admiration and respect of such a legendary man as the Gunsmith.

THIRTY

It wasn't the best Christmas, but Clint had known worse. Pete had finally been persuaded to have himself carried downstairs and propped up in a chair beside the bar. They tied him in his seat because he might have fallen out after he'd drunk too much whiskey and that would cause him embarrassment. Pete's girls had talked a few of the boys into going into the hills to chop down a tree, then drag it in, and set it up near the piano.

The best part of the day had been when most everybody took advantage of Pete's generosity and free liquor. While they drank, they decorated the tree. They tied empty beer bottles, buttons, and colored paper and then popped corn and made strings to loop around and around. The piano player was good and he played some favorite Christmas songs and the singing was loud and exuberant.

Presents were exchanged. Clint got a new Stetson from Kathy who had the eye of every man in the place from the moment she'd entered the room. Pete's girls tried to ignore her, but they were the only ones who did. Their jealousy got the better of them and they agreed that their Christmas present to everyone would be a free ride upstairs. Then, they got all the attention they wanted but weren't seen much for the rest of the afternoon.

Clint presented Kathy with a small, pearl-handled derringer, a beautiful piece of work that he had restored himself so that it was better than when it was made.

"It's fitting," she said, "that the Gunsmith should give me a gun."

"You've got everything else, Kathy. Besides, you saved my life on that train with a gun; maybe this one will save yours one day." As they looked appreciatively at each other, the piano player started a waltz.

"Would you waltz with me?"

"Now?"

She looked so offended and hurt, Clint quickly added, "Sure I will!" He took her in his arms. Her hair was tied on the top of her head and she had never looked more radiant or beautiful. She was as light as a breeze in his arms and danced as if born to it.

"We make a lovely couple, Clint. Everyone is watching us."

"They are watching you," he said, knowing it was true. "And since you started this, the line will be twenty deep."

"What's going to happen with us, Clint? Do you think you can settle down here and we can get married? I just know my business will prosper."

"Kathy," he said gently, "you're trying to saddle the wrong horse. I'm just not marrying material. I told you that already. I can't change."

She bit her lip. "Yeah," she sniffled, "I guess I knew you were going to say that. Clint?"

"Yes?"

"Have you seen that girl that Zeb is so taken with?"

He smiled a little in spite of himself. "Why do you ask?"

"Just wondering. Is she pretty?"

"Gorgeous," he lied. "Face like an angel, breasts as big as . . ." He could not keep from laughing out loud.

"What's so damned funny!"

"You," he said. "If you are interested in Zeb Haywood,

come right out and say so. Don't beat around the bush and play games."

"Well, I wouldn't be if you were the marrying kind, Clint. But next to you, Zeb is the only one in Raton who interests me. This Wadsworth business, is that serious?"

His smile vanished. "I'm afraid so. They are coming to kill Zeb."

"But he's a gunfighter like yourself. I heard him say that he's fast and unafraid. I admire his courage and he certainly has . . . well, a lot of flair."

"That he does."

"Then, he'll probably have to kill those men?"

Clint frowned. "Kathy," he said, chosing his words slowly, "it might not be that easy. Zeb is a little bit overconfident."

"You mean he could get shot!"

"It happens to the best of us."

"Oh, damn! You will help him, won't you?"

"That's what I came for."

"Good." She was obviously greatly relieved. When the music ended and a line of men stepped forward to claim the next dance, Kathy whispered, "Take me to Rosie's Place. I want to see Zeb."

"You can't go in there. It's a whorehouse!"

"I don't intend to solicit work. Just to visit Zeb."

She was serious. "All right," Clint said, "let's go."

Zeb was in the saloon downstairs sitting with Susie and several other girls. When Clint escorted Kathy into the room, the place went dead silent. To Clint's way of thinking, they were just about as welcome as a polecat at a picnic.

"What are you doing here?" Zeb asked, rushing over to them. "My God, Gunsmith, don't you know any better than to bring your woman into a place like this!"

"I'm not his woman," Kathy said after inspecting Susie

and finding her to be no competition. "In fact, Clint has just informed me that he will be leaving Raton one of these days. So I . . . well, I was thinking that this is Christmas and your father may not be around for the next one and that maybe you and I should stay close to him today. It might be something you'll look back on in later years and be glad of."

Zeb swallowed. "You know," he said quietly, "you are absolutely right, Miss Ault. You, me, and the Gunsmith are the ones he loves the most. I feel like a fool for not seeing that on my own. I'm grateful to you, Miss Ault."

She linked her arm through his and smiled right into his eyes. "You can start calling me Kathy."

They headed for the door and Clint followed. When he looked back, Susie was on her feet and a full bottle of whiskey was coming at him as she screamed. "You tell him never to come back! That's *my* Christmas present!"

Clint dodged the bottle, which shattered against the wall. "I'll tell him, Susie, but I don't think it'll be necessary."

THIRTY-ONE

Clint felt good seeing the way old Pete Haywood seemed to light up when he saw his boy and Kathy walk in the door of the Hot Lizard arm in arm. He ordered drinks on the house, which was rather meaningless since they had been all day.

Motioning Clint over, Pete said, "Are you sure you want my son cozying up to your woman that way? Clint, I wouldn't want you to get sore."

"I'm not going to get sore, Pete. Kathy is the marrying kind and I told her that I just was not. I think we'll stay close friends but . . ."

"How close?"

"Kathy will be moving out of my room after today, I suspect. I think she has her sights set dead center on Zeb."

"Hot damn! That is exactly the kind of woman I have been hoping he'd find. Look at the two of them together! Don't they look fine?"

"They sure do," Clint said, "and unless I miss my guess, this clown with all the silver conchos and leather fringes walking in the door must be Texas Jack."

Pete scowled. "I was hoping he would have froze out on the prairie this past week. Yeah, that's him all right. Biggest phony and braggart in New Mexico. I can't stand the arrogant bastard."

The man waved to everyone and then began to pump hands. He was big, well over six feet, and had a florid face.

His hair was graying around the temples and he had a paunch that hung over an enormous buckle of polished silver. Almost every chubby finger had a big silver and turquoise ring on it, and his leather coat had long fringes hanging off the arms. He wore silver spurs, big ones like the vaqueros use, and he'd cinched them down low so that when he walked, the rowels rolled along the floor making him sound like a piece of moving machinery. His hat had a wide brim and was as white as cream. It had a big hatband of leather and more conchos, each one polished to a luster. He wore not one, but two guns, butts forward for a crossdraw that had to tie up his fat arms like pretzels.

"The man looks like a fool, doesn't he?" Pete growled. "And when he opens his mouth, he proves it."

"He's a strutting, overstuffed, over-the-hill peacock. Why do these people listen to him?"

"He does know a lot about gunfighters," Pete grumped. "The man is almost an encyclopedia of knowledge on 'em. Billy the Kid, Cody, Earp, me, and the Gunsmith. He knows all about us."

"How?"

"Hell if I know. But he does. If you question him close, you can't trip the man up. He does know his stuff. He knows more about me than I do!"

"Hmmm, well, I think I'll go over and meet him. He may know the facts and figures, but he damn sure doesn't know much about the real art of gunfighting. He has that boy of yours fanning his gun."

"I know." Pete sighed. "I saw it first when I was hiding in that barrel. Couldn't believe my eyes!"

"Neither could I yesterday," Clint said. "The simple fact of the matter is that we have to straighten this Texas Jack out before he gets Zeb killed. I'll bet anything that he's the one who has been feeding him all those foolish ideas about becoming a famous gunfighter.''

"Guess I ought to kill him," Pete said. "Before he gets my boy killed. Thing of it is, he's promised to face the Wadsworths and help Zeb.

"Zeb told me he doesn't want any help."

"Zeb considers Texas Jack to be about the best friend he has in this world. If I killed him, or you ran him off, Zeb wouldn't forgive either of us. Whatever the man says, Zeb believes is gospel."

"Have you tried to tell him that no real gunfighter would be caught dead dressed like that?"

"No," Pete said quietly, "I always thought the less I said about guns and killing men with them the better it would be for my son. That was my mistake. By the time I realized I should have been answering his questions, it was too late. Texas Jack had taken my place. And now that I'm dying, there ain't one hell of a lot I can do."

Clint nodded. He had talked to the doctor who was seeing Pete and the man had convinced him that Pete was dying. The paralysis seemed to be creeping upward and inward and there wasn't a thing in the world anyone could do to help. Pete would not last until the next spring.

"I'll go have a word with this man," Clint said.

"I'll tell him a few facts of life and advise him to keep his mouth shut when it comes to Zeb and his becoming famous."

"You can try."

"I'll do whatever is necessary, Pete."

Clint finished his drink and moved across the bar. Zeb Haywood wasn't capable of becoming fast on the draw, and the sooner he realized it and got this gunfighting nonsense out of his system, the better his chances were of living to a ripe old age. Maybe marry Kathy and have some children who would go on to become civic leaders and doctors and even senators.

Texas Jack stood in the way of all that, though Zeb couldn't see it clearly yet. Texas Jack and the Wadsworths who had been released from prison and were coming to Raton. Clint's expression was grim. This man first, then the Wadsworths and then he'd stick around to see old Pete was buried proper. After that . . . well, he was going to climb on Duke and ride a long, long ways.

"So I walked right up to Wild Bill Hickok, and even though I knew he was madder'n hell, I told him just what I thought about the way he'd handled things and then I let him decide what his next move was going to be. I was ready for anything."

Clint said, "So you knew Wild Bill Hickok, did you?"

Texas Jack stopped talking. He smiled broadly and stuck out his hand with all the silver and turquoise. "Yes, sir, and I do know all about you, too, Gunsmith. It is an honor! A real, genuine honor to finally make your acquaintance after all these years."

Clint ignored the hand. It was withdrawn and the smile on the man's face had turned to an expression that was hostile and guarded.

"Did I offend you in some way?" Texas Jack asked quietly.

"Not yet, except for the way you are dressed and what you have been telling young Zeb. I think you and I had better step outside alone."

"I don't want to draw on you! I'm through with killing!"

Clint grabbed him by the fringes and propelled him out the door. "Cut the crap, Jack. No one is listening. I want you to tell Zeb that he's no gunfighter and neither are you."

"That'd be a lie," he whispered hoarsely. "A lie!"

"No, it wouldn't. You may have fooled all those fellas inside. I don't know where you got so much information on gunfighters and I don't care. The point I'm making is that your stories are starting to become dangerous. They already could have got Zeb killed once and he might not be lucky to escape next time.''

"Luck had nothing to do with it! Zeb outdrew Elmer Wadsworth and shot him dead in the street. Elmer was a real gunman. I have taught Zeb the art, the science if you will, of gunfighting. He has—''

Clint had heard more than enough. He grabbed the man by the shirt and dragged him up on his toes. ''You're a phony. Now, you make Zeb see that he is no gunfighter, or I swear I'll run you out of this country with your tail between your fat legs. Your choice. Which is it?''

Texas Jack was sweating heavily though the air was freezing. ''Listen''—he swallowed and licked his lips—''it's Christmas, the time of fellowship. Can't we—''

''No,'' Clint said, ''we can't be friends. Not now and not tomorrow. You're a dangerous man with dangerous ideas that get people killed. It stops right now, Jack, or you and I are going to show the people of Raton just what a fake you really are.''

''All right! All right! You win. I'll talk to Zeb. But what am I supposed to say? That he has no chance at all of killing the Wadsworths? That he should run? You know he won't believe even me. What do you want me to say, Gunsmith? Tell me!''

''Tell him that he needs to start thinking of using a shotgun. I will get him one and teach him how to handle it. Also, he needs a decent gun with a sight and a trigger that works. I want him to stop fanning the hammer. You can tell him all that for starters.''

Texas Jack nodded forlornly. ''I will,'' he said, ''but he might not listen.''

''Make him listen, Jack. We are running out of time.''

THIRTY-TWO

"They're here!"

Clint stood up and checked his gun. He looked at the man who stood in the doorway of the Hot Lizard and said, "How many?"

"Five."

"You sure?"

"Yes, sir! I'm on my way to find Zeb now. He's—"

"He rented a buckboard and took Miss Ault south for a ride to look at some antiques they might buy. He won't be back until late this afternoon."

"But . . . but at least let me go find Texas Jack!"

Clint smiled with great amusement. "Somehow, I don't think that is possible. I think he's probably hiding under some bed."

"You can't face them alone."

Clint patted his gun. "I'm not alone. I got this on my hip and that is all the company I need."

The man just nodded. "They said they were coming down to meet Zeb, and that if he ran, they'd just chase him down."

Zeb's no coward; he's still just a little bit too proud and a bit foolish, Clint thought. He did not know if Texas Jack had really tried to talk some sense into Zeb or not, but the young man hadn't been willing to learn how to use a shotgun—he'd considered it an insult. Furthermore, he'd gotten so angry he hadn't even been talking to Clint. Mostly, he was spending his time with Kathy. It looked like a match for certain and Clint hoped they'd marry before Pete died.

Fred the bartender grabbed a shotgun from behind the bar. "I can't let you face them alone," he said with grim determination. "I'm going out there with you."

"No, you're not, but thanks for the offer. If any get past me, you be standing behind the bar with that aimed waist high. It'll be your chance then."

Fred swallowed noisily. "I sure hope it doesn't come to that. But if it does, you can die knowing they'll be taken care of before they have a chance to get to young Zeb."

"You're a good and a loyal man and I wish I knew you better."

"There will be time afterward, Gunsmith. You can take them."

"I'm bettin' on it, Fred." They poured two whiskeys and they saluted each other in silence. It was good, Clint thought, to know that even if he failed to stop all of them, which seemed highly unlikely, that Fred was ready to finish his business.

"They're coming down the street now! All walking side by side!"

Clint set his glass down, turned, then started for the door.

"Good luck!" Fred whispered, breaking open the shotgun and putting in fresh shells.

"A little luck won't hurt at all," Clint said as he stepped outside.

They were still a good two blocks away, but coming they were. Whatever wagon and horse traffic there'd been on the street was funneling into alleys and sidestreets to get out of the line of fire. By the time Clint reached the middle of the street, it was empty except for the men he faced.

Clint knew nothing about these men, not how fast they were or anything. He did know that at least two had been in prison up until Christmas, so they could not be too practiced with their guns. He hoped they were downright rusty. One of them looked like a professional gunfighter; he was a tall man with a tied-down holster and he was wearing a black suit with a red bandanna knotted around his throat. He was the man Clint decided he would have to kill first if he were to have any hope of getting the others.

"That's far enough," Clint said.

"We are looking for Zeb Haywood," the gunfighter said. "We got no quarrel with you, Gunsmith. Why don't you leave this one be? Even you can't take five of us."

"Probably not," he answered, "but I aim to try."

"That's a damn shame," the man said. "I wasn't planning on facing you."

"Then ride out of here while you can," Clint said easily.

"Can't. This is a blood feud. Have to find Zeb and kill him."

"Then, you have to go through me first," Clint said, positioning himself to draw. "I guess the talking is over."

"Guess so."

The man made his play and his hand moved like the strike of a rattlesnake—a blur that went for his sixgun just as Clint's hand did. Two guns came up and then both exploded, but one sent a bullet into the dirt and one sent a bullet through a man's chest.

Clint spun around and dropped to one knee as a rifle began to boom over the street. One of the Wadsworth brothers yelled and fired up at old Pete Haywood, who had somehow dragged himself out of his deathbed to hang over the windowsill with a rifle propped up in his arms. Pete fired twice and two men went down before he was riddled in a volley of gunfire.

But that momentary distraction was all that Clint needed. His gun was smoking and every shot scored as men fell and then lay twitching and writhing in the dirt.

When his gun was empty, Clint looked up at the second story window and saw Pete hanging face down against the outer wall. Clint did not have to go upstairs to know that his old friend was dead. But damn it, he had died cleanly and gloriously and quickly as a man should!

Clint knuckled his eyes dry and reloaded his gun. Pete had died to save him and his son. He must have felt damned good about that as the first bullet hit him. Damned good.

THIRTY-THREE

They buried Pete with most of the town attending the funeral. Rosie was there, but Susie wasn't and it was just as well because Zeb wouldn't have seen her anyway. The preacher said some fine things about Pete, and Clint thought his old friend would have been pleased by the turnout and how everyone admitted he'd been one of Raton's leading citizens.

So the Hot Lizard and a whole bunch more prime real estate would become Zeb's and it looked as if he would live to enjoy the fruits of his father's labors. Clint felt good about that. Given time, Zeb would gain strength and wisdom. Kathy would see to it.

He was ready to leave. The weather was clear but cold and he was thinking of Arizona and packing his gear. Duke was fat and sassy and plenty eager to travel.

"Clint!"

He was saddling Duke when Kathy flew in the door. "Clint!"

One look at her face told him that there was something very, very wrong. The first thing he thought of was that more of the Wadsworths were coming. "What's wrong?"

She was crying and damn near hysterical and that just wasn't the Kathy he had come to know and grudgingly admire. He had never quite resolved in his own mind if she'd played any part in the killing of her banker husband, but he

was willing to give her the benefit of the doubt and hope that
Zeb treated her right.

"It's Zeb! He's coming to kill you!"

"What!"

"He's coming. He's been looking for you all over town!"

"But why?"

"Texas Jack! That damn Texas Jack told him that he saw
you let old Pete take the first bullets and only then did you
have the nerve to return fire."

"The liar!" Clint could not believe his own ears.

"I know, I know! And then he managed to get Zeb to
believing that you'd told everyone in town that Zeb had run
away rather than face the Wadsworths. And that you had
been forced to do his killing for him."

Kathy choked. "Clint, he's convinced Zeb that you've
told everyone that he is a coward!"

"Well, talk to him!"

"I tried," she shrieked. "He won't listen. He says he is
going to prove once and for all that he's not a coward and that
he'll outdraw and wound you for allowing his father to be
killed."

Clint groaned. "Outdraw and wound me, huh? Prove to
everyone that he is faster than the Gunsmith."

Clint scrubbed his face with his hand. He could not run, yet
he couldn't possibly kill Pete's son. What a mess! The kid
was a complete fool, and when this was over, Clint resolved
to find that damn Texas Jack and strip his hide off with a dull
knife.

"Listen, I'll just finish up and ride out," Clint said tiredly.
"Let Zeb, and whoever else wants to, believe that I was
running."

"Hold it! Get away from him, Kathy!"

"Zeb, no!"

He was standing, legs spread wide, in the doorway. His

hand was poised over his gun. ''Whenever you are ready, Gunsmith, I am.''

''Don't be a fool,'' Clint said tightly. ''Texas Jack lied.''

Zeb shook his head. ''Ever since you arrived, you've tried to make me look bad—tried any way you could to make me bolt and run. Then, you fought my battle, only you propped my father up with a rifle to even the odds in your favor.''

''There were five of them! Pete took out two and I got the rest, including a gunslinger they hired.''

''After all of it, you spread the story about me running out and being a coward. Now, I'm going to correct the story.''

Clint took a deep breath. He had had enough of this fool and it was a waste of his time and breath to try to explain things anymore. ''Go ahead, Zeb, you're calling the play. Let's see how you really stack up against a gunfighter.''

Zeb drew. Clint waited until the young man's gun was coming up and then he drew very deliberately and shot Zeb in his gunhand.

Zeb cried out in pain and his pistol went flying as he grabbed his wrist to try to stanch the flow of blood. Baring his teeth, he said, ''Go ahead and finish me off! I'll never be a gunfighter now, not with this.''

''You never were a gunfighter and never would have been, Zeb.''

While Kathy fussed over him, Clint finished saddling his horse and then mounted and rode past.

''Clint!''

He turned in the saddle to see Kathy hurrying after him. She was crying and smiling at the same time. ''What?''

''Thank you for saving his life. Thank you for this time and all the other times.''

Clint's anger washed out of him and he grinned. ''You take care of him. Drill some sense into his stupid head and turn him into the kind of man his father would have been proud of—the kind of man he has the stuff to become.''

"I will,'' she vowed. "I love him very much, Clint. It isn't just his money.''

"I didn't figure it was.''

"Will you ever come back? I want to name our first son after you.''

"Then, I'll come back.'' He tipped his hat. "Right now, though, I've got some unfinished business to attend to.''

"Texas Jack?''

"Yep. I won't kill him, and he's broken no laws so that I can't even see him go to prison, but when I'm done with him, Kathy, he'll never return to bother you or Zeb again.''

She beamed. "I still love you, too, Clint!''

Clint rode away whistling a tune. He would find that meddling fake Texas Jack and tie a rope around his neck and drag him all the way to Arizona. By the time they arrived, Clint figured Jack would have a whole new attitude about life and gunfighters.

But it would be one story that the flashy old phony would be too embarrassed to tell.

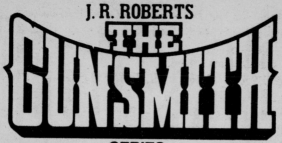

J. R. ROBERTS
THE GUNSMITH

SERIES

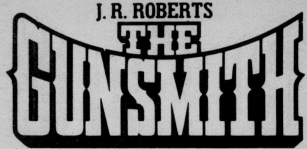

J. R. ROBERTS
THE GUNSMITH

SERIES

Prices may be slightly higher in Canada.

Available at your local bookstore or return this form to:

CHARTER BOOKS
Book Mailing Service
P.O. Box 690, Rockville Centre, NY 11571

Please send me the titles checked above. I enclose _____. Include 75¢ for postage and handling if one book is ordered; 25¢ per book for two or more not to exceed $1.75. California, Illinois, New York and Tennessee residents please add sales tax.

NAME_____

ADDRESS_____

CITY_____STATE/ZIP_____

(allow six weeks for delivery.)   **A1/a**